SEAGLASS SUMMER

Also by Anjali Banerjee

Maya Running

Looking for Bapu

SEAGLASS SUMMER

ANjALi BANerJee

A YEARLING BOOK

Sale of this book without a front cover may be unauthorized.
If the book is coverless, it may have been reported to the publisher as "unsold or destroyed"
and neither the author nor the publisher may have received payment for it.

This is a work of fiction. Names, characters, places, and incidents either are
the product of the author's imagination or are used fictitiously. Any resemblance
to actual persons, living or dead, events, or locales is entirely coincidental.

Text copyright © 2010 by Anjali Banerjee
Cover art and interior illustrations copyright © 2010 by Ann Boyajian

All rights reserved. Published in the United States by Yearling, an imprint of
Random House Children's Books, a division of Random House, Inc., New York. Originally
published in hardcover in the United States by Wendy Lamb Books, an imprint of
Random House Children's Books, a division of Random House, Inc., New York, in 2010.

Yearling and the jumping horse design are registered trademarks of Random House, Inc.

Visit us on the Web! www.randomhouse.com/kids

Educators and librarians, for a variety of teaching tools, visit us at
www.randomhouse.com/teachers

The Library of Congress has cataloged the hardcover edition of this work as follows:
Banerjee, Anjali.
Seaglass summer / Anjali Banerjee. — 1st ed.
p. cm.
Summary: While spending a month on an island off the coast of Washington
helping in her Uncle Sanjay's veterinary clinic, eleven-year-old Poppy Ray soon
questions her decision to follow in her uncle's footsteps.
ISBN 978-0-385-73567-4 (hc) — ISBN 978-0-385-90555-8 (lib. bdg.) —
ISBN 978-0-375-89666-8 (ebook)
[1. Veterinarians—Fiction. 2. Pets—Fiction. 3. Uncles—Fiction.
4. East Indian Americans—Fiction. 5. Washington (State)—Fiction.] I. Title.
PZ7.B22155Se 2010
[Fic]—dc22
2009025468

ISBN 978-0-375-84399-0 (pbk.)

Printed in the United States of America
10 9 8 7 6 5

First Yearling Edition 2011

Random House Children's Books supports the First Amendment
and celebrates the right to read.

In memory of
our beloved, sweet cat,
Monet, 1999–2009

Chapter One
TO THE ISLAND

Move over, Dr. Dolittle.

I, Poppy Ray, age eleven, am on a mission to heal all the animals at my uncle's clinic. Mom and Dad are off to India on business, but I'm not going this time. I love curries, Bengali sweets, and my cousins, but I don't love being cooped up indoors during the monsoon floods. I convinced my parents I'd be better off with Uncle Sanjay this summer, even if he lives on a faraway island in Washington State. He's our only relative in North

America, and he loves me to death because I love animals. How could he say no?

So that's how I found myself leaving everything I knew behind—Los Angeles smog, traffic, and all my friends— and boarding an airplane for a strange new place. After two hours, we're about to land in Seattle, on the edge of the Northwest sea. As we drop through the clouds, I press my nose to the window. I've never been this far north, where mountains rise around us like giant Sno-Kones, where sparkling rivers run through a city of glittering high-rises. On the harbor between Seattle and the mountains, ferryboats, freighters, and cruise ships glide through the waves. Hundreds of green dots float in the distance. Which one is my uncle's island? What if I get lost on the way?

We land and hurry through baggage claim and out into the sunshine and cool breeze. A Yellow Cab carries us through the hilly city to the waterfront, and then Mom and Dad rush me up a hundred concrete steps and into the ferry building. Dad hauls my giant purple suitcase, which holds my most precious belongings—my clothes, my fifth-grade yearbook, and my veterinarian first-aid kit. I saved up six months' allowance to buy just the right one, complete with tongue depressors, cotton swabs, a stethoscope, a digital thermometer, and a blanket wrap. These aren't the kid versions. They're the real thing. I'm serious about becoming an animal doctor, just like my uncle. I even took pictures of the label on the clear plastic carrying case. In big black letters are the words "Deluxe First-Aid Kit for Animals." I sent the photos to my relatives, and I brought the kit to school. My friends kept bending the flexible thermometer, made for pet safety. I can't wait to show the kit to my uncle.

At the top of the stairs, Mom hugs me and says, "Oh, Poppy, I wish we could take you all the way to the island, but our plane left late. We can't miss our connecting flight to Mumbai. We have to see you off here."

And you could be coming with us if you hadn't been so stubborn. That is what she doesn't say. But she sighs. My mother is an expert in the sigh department.

"I'll be fine," I say, and it comes out way too chirpy. I'll be perfectly okay on my own. This is what I wanted. So why is my throat dry?

Mom sighs again. "Uncle Sanjay will be waiting for you at the Nisqually Island stop. The ferry worker will stay with you. See that woman over there?"

A powerful-looking blond lady waves at us. I bet she could push the boat all by herself. But she's wearing a soft pink jacket, like a puff of cotton candy.

I wave back, pretending to be brave. "Don't worry. I've got everything I need."

Mom's eyes mist and she hugs me again. "We'll miss

you. You can still come to India with us. We could try to get you on a flight."

"No!" I say. She'd do it, too.

"Okay, okay," she says. "You could still go to wilderness camp with Emma and Anna—"

"I'm staying with Uncle Sanjay," I say. Emma and Anna Chen are identical twins, my very best friends. I promised to buy them postcards and presents on the island.

"Be good at Uncle Sanjay's," Mom says. "We'll pick you up at his place. It's about time we saw his house."

I've wanted to visit him ever since he moved to the island four years ago, but he lives with a large furry dog and Mom is allergic to anything with fur. We could stay in a motel, but we haven't had the chance so far. He visits us often in L.A., bringing gifts made in Washington— Seattle chocolates, huckleberry jam, or Walla Walla onions. He takes me for walks and tells funny stories about the animals that come into his clinic.

"I hope you'll have fun with the cats and dogs," Mom says, being nice even though the thought of pets makes her queasy.

"Thanks, Mom," I say.

Maybe it's the people jostling by to get on the ferry. Maybe it's the mournful honking of waterbirds. But for some reason, a twinge of worry prods at my ribs. I've never ridden a ferry before. I've never been away from my parents for a whole month. First time for everything, I tell myself. I'm not a baby anymore.

Mom gives me a Suffocation Cuddle. I breathe in the lavender scent of her hair. She blurs at close range—the dimple on her cheek, her tea-colored skin, the paint stains under her fingernails. The artwork she wears all over her—the earrings she made from beads, the bells that serve as buttons on her homemade floral-print shirt—jingles and clinks.

Dad squeezes my hand. Suddenly, I don't want to let go. "Have you got everything, Poppykins? Cell phone in case of emergency?"

I nod. I can't speak. Dad is always organized, just like me. In my bedroom at home, I line up my animal books on the top shelf, and on the second shelf, I keep trophies for spelling and the science fair. In my closet, my jeans are on one side, my shirts on the other. I make my bed and vacuum almost every day. For a split second, I miss my room. I wonder where I'll sleep at Uncle Sanjay's house.

"If you don't get a signal, call from Uncle's home phone," Mom says. "We'll also try to call you."

If I don't get a signal? But I get a signal everywhere.

"Have you got your gum boots?" Dad asks, letting go of my hand.

He means rain boots. He still uses a few words from India.

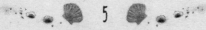

"I have my blue ones."

"Don't get off the ferry before Nisqually Island," Mom says. "Listen to the ferry lady."

"I promise."

Dad flips open his wallet. "Did we give you enough emergency cash?"

I shake my purse. "It's all in here."

Mom hugs me again, and I hang on a moment too long.

The ferry lady comes over. "We'd better go." She leads me down the ramp. She tries to chat, but I can't talk for the frog jumping in my throat. The boat engine hums. I glance back at Mom, her frizzy black hair blowing in the wind; and at Dad, in his pressed blue suit, holding her hand. As I board the ferry, I can still see my parents' dark eyes watching me from the dock.

Chapter Two
A BUMP IN THE ROAD

On the voyage to Nisqually Island, I watch for killer whales hiding beneath the ocean waves. The ride is calm and smooth. The sea lifts hilly green-black islands; small boats pass with their flapping white sails, and two sea lions rest on a buoy, watching me. I wonder what they think of a skinny girl with tangled black hair and eyes the gold color of sunset. Do they have dreams? Wishes?

Halfway across the water, when the mist rolls in and the

air turns cool and salty, my cell phone signal disappears. The ocean spreads out on all sides. I don't know which way is home. A touch of panic rises in my chest. I've never been alone in a strange place, except once when I was little and Mom lost me at Disneyland. I cried at the top of my lungs—I thought she was gone forever—but then she came running and grabbed my hand. I must've been lost for only a minute, but it felt like a year.

After a while, the ferry lady comes over and sits next to me. She smells like french fries. "So what do you have planned for the summer?" she asks.

"I plan to save the animals on Nisqually Island." I sit up straight and take a deep breath. "I'm going to work at the Furry Friends Animal Clinic."

"Is that so?" Her nose twitches. "Good for you. Nisqually is my favorite place to visit. You can drive the whole length, top to bottom, in about an hour. Boats, seagulls, beaches—the island is beautiful. Holds many surprises. Look, there it is." She points out the window.

The island creeps toward us. I imagined bright flowers and cute bungalows perched along the shoreline, and happy dogs running on the beach. But instead, a dense forest covers the hillsides all the way down to the water. I don't see any buildings. What if my uncle lives in a tree house? I'm heading into the uncharted wilderness. I could turn around now, go to India with my parents. I could dive into the water and swim back . . .

No, that's silly. Uncle Sanjay lives in a house in a town, probably on the other side of the island. His address is 25 Sitka Spruce Road, Witless Cove, on Nisqually Island, in Washington State.

The boat docks with a thud and the passengers sweep me to the exit doors. I nearly lose my suitcase as I stumble down the narrow ramp into a parking lot. My heart pounds, but I stride forward, pretending to know where I'm going. Lines of cars are parked in rows facing the ferry, waiting to board. Ahead of me are a square gray building with a sign, NISQUALLY LANDING, and a two-lane road that disappears into the forest.

The ferry lady stays close to me as I watch for Uncle Sanjay. I have his number in my purse, but I can't get a cell phone signal. I keep checking my watch. What if he doesn't come?

I wait and wait, and then a noisy, dented red pickup truck rattles into the parking lot and belches a few times before pulling to a stop. A tall man gets out of the truck. Uncle Sanjay. Someone else, a dark shape bouncing up and down, waits in the passenger seat.

"There's my uncle," I say, pointing at the man.

"Okay, hon," the ferry lady says. "You have a good time with your furry friends." Then she is gone.

Uncle Sanjay runs toward me, his feet pointing out

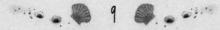

sideways. He's a tall, hazelnut brown version of Mom—same wide forehead and huge interested eyes.

"My dearest niece, I'm sorry I'm late!" He hugs me so hard he lifts me off my feet. He smells of wood smoke and spice.

"I was getting worried," I say.

"A Jack Russell terrier came in with garbage gut. We had to pump his stomach, and I fell behind on my schedule." He grabs the handle of my suitcase.

Poor little dog. "Will he be okay?"

"Garbage gut can be dangerous, but he'll be fine. Come come, let's go." Uncle Sanjay wheels my suitcase toward the truck. A bumper sticker on the back reads GEODUCK FOR STATE BIRD. I picture a giant island duck chasing me, flapping its wings.

Furry Friends Animal Clinic is painted in bright blue on each side of the truck. Inside, a huge yellow dog jumps up and down.

Uncle Sanjay taps on the window. "That's Stu. He still acts like a puppy." He throws my suitcase into the back. It lands with a whump. He slams the tailgate a few times to keep it closed, then yanks open the passenger-side door.

Stu charges out and leaps at me, knocking me back into the grass. He sits on top of me, paws on my shoulders. Floppy ears dangle in my face.

I scrunch up my nose. "Help! I'm suffocating. Stu, stop it!" But he doesn't listen.

"Stu!" Uncle Sanjay says from far away. "Leave your cousin Poppy alone."

Cousin? I am *not* the dog's cousin. Stu breathes hot doggy breath on my cheeks.

"Stu, bad dog. Get off me!" I shout, but Stu keeps drooling and licking my face.

Uncle Sanjay laughs—a rolling roar. "Stay calm—"

"Calm? How can I be calm with a giant dog in my face?"

"Studebaker Chatterji, come."

Studebaker? The dog lumbers up and leaps into the truck. I climb in next to him. I'm turning into a pancake, squished against the door. Stu rests his paws on my lap.

"Sorry about the mess," Uncle Sanjay says cheerfully. He shoves junk onto the floor.

As the truck rumbles to life, he pats the dashboard. "I've had this hump of tin since my early days as a vet in Virginia. Drove across the country and it has not failed me yet."

"Don't you mean *hunk* of tin?" I hold on to the door handle.

"That's what I said." He presses the pedal with his foot and the truck wobbles down the narrow road. Tall trees bend their branches low, forming a tunnel of green above us. There isn't much traffic, but everyone who passes us waves. Uncle Sanjay waves back. Nobody waves in L.A. unless they're angry at you, and they usually wave one finger, not a whole hand.

"How was the ferry ride?" he says as he speeds along. He waggles his forefinger at me. "The boat stops at only a few of these islands, nah? There are many more islands. Some are invisible at high tide. Water rises up and covers them completely."

"Invisible islands?" I don't want to sound too interested, but my mouth drops open.

"Well, you can see them underwater." He grins. "Nisqually Island is always visible, however. It's bigger than you'd think. Many beaches and parks. Swifty Bay, Witless Cove Beach, Humphrey Landing. And we have three towns, too, not only Witless Cove. Lopty Village and Freetown."

"Wow, three whole towns." I won't have time to explore. I'll be too busy with the animals. "When do we go to work?"

"Tomorrow. The clinic is closed on Sunday afternoon." The truck rattles and creaks, but we don't slow down, even when the road twists around curves or climbs hills or crashes through puddles. Rain fell in the night; puddles are everywhere, reflecting the sky and trees.

"Oops, water in the road." Uncle Sanjay spins the

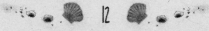

steering wheel. The truck veers and skids through a stream. I hear a loud clunk, some bumping, and a couple of thuds. I glance in the side mirror. Bright colors flap away behind the truck. My suitcase bounces along the road, snapped open, spitting out my clothes, my shoes, and my underwear—right into the rushing stream.

Chapter three
ISLAND GEAR

"Uncle Sanjay, stop! My suitcase fell out!"

Uncle Sanjay glances in the rearview mirror. "Oh, my dear niece." He pulls over to the shoulder, and the three of us scramble out of the truck. Uncle Sanjay scratches his head. "Must get that tailgate fixed."

"It's *broken*? And you put my *suitcase* back there?"

"Nowhere else to put it. I could've strapped it to the hood, I suppose."

I take off my shoes and socks, roll up my jeans, and

wade into the stream. Icy water laps over my feet. Uncle Sanjay follows to help search for my clothes. Stu leaps around, splashing us. I find my pants, shirts, and socks, all soggy. Stu chomps one of my T-shirts.

Uncle Sanjay grabs the shirt. "Stu, no eating. Bad for you."

I catch my sneakers before they float away, and my yearbook.

"What am I going to wear?" I say. Where is my vet kit? The stream rushes more loudly, bubbling in my ears.

"Not to worry. We'll buy you some clothes. Nothing much is open today, except the Trading Post, if we get there soon. You'll find some good solid gear. Island gear."

Island gear? I start to shiver. Cars whiz by, people waving from the windows. I'm too upset to wave back. I try to remember my bedroom at home and the way my clothes used to be, folded neatly and dry.

Uncle Sanjay grabs the soaking, broken carrying case. Cotton swabs and tongue depressors are floating downstream.

I catch my stethoscope and thermometer before they sink. "The water ruined everything! I saved up for that kit. What am I going to do?"

His eyebrows rise. "You bought the kit for your trip to the island?" His lips are pressed together, as if he's trying not to laugh.

I snatch the container from him. "It's cracked now. And there goes the blanket wrap!"

"Not to worry. We have the proper equipment at the clinic." He pats my back.

"But this was *my* kit. I put my name on it in Magic Marker, right there."

"Ah, I see. Well, keep the box. Perhaps you'll fill it with something new. Come, let's go."

How could I ever fill it with anything but emergency veterinary supplies?

We climb back into the truck. I try to send 911 text messages to Mom, but I still can't get a signal. The deeper Uncle Sanjay drives into the shadowy woods, the slower the world moves, as if time skips Nisqually Island and races on through to Seattle.

But then we burst out into the sunshine, next to the shoreline. A wooden sign appears, half covered by twisty madrone branches: WELCOME TO WITLESS COVE.

"Where did that name come from?" I ask Uncle Sanjay.

"In the early 1800s, when the Wilkes Expedition sailed through these islands, Captain Wilkes found this cove shallow and exposed to storms, useless for boats wanting to come ashore or drop anchor here. Scared sailors 'witless.' Wilkes coined the name Witless Cove."

He points to the right, to a curved, sandy ribbon of shore littered with rocks and driftwood. The black ocean throws up huge white-capped waves, and the smells of kelp and sea salt waft into my nose. Stu whines as we pass the beach.

"You can find many treasures there," Uncle Sanjay goes on. "Quartz, shells, seaglass. Stu likes to go exploring."

I want to stop at the beach right away, but Uncle Sanjay turns left, away from the water and into town. No mall, no painted lines in the road. No fast-food restaurants. I bet nobody here has heard of a traffic light. People are biking and strolling along brick sidewalks. What's with all the smiling and waving? Uncle Sanjay must be famous in this village of old-fashioned lampposts, shops, and hanging flowerpots. A rusty fire truck sits in the overgrown driveway of an old white church. I have to admit, Witless Cove is pretty, but nothing can fix my broken suitcase or my first aid kit, and I'm still in desperate need of a telephone.

In one blink, we pass the main street and pull up at a square building made of giant logs. A wooden sign reads, THE WITLESS COVE TRADING POST. I have to buy clothes in *there*? When Uncle Sanjay and I get out, Stu moves into the driver's seat. He looks like a proud human disguised as a dog.

Inside the store, families in jeans and T-shirts mix with people in fancy clothes. They browse the soaps, lotions, and displays of cockleshells and colorful chunks of

seaglass. Up front, a few women chat about a clambake and a Girl Scout Cookie sale.

I choose a few island postcards for Emma and Anna. I wonder what they're doing at summer camp. They're into fashion. They would never let me shop for clothes *here*, in this world of polyester pants and shirts with sequined bunnies on the front.

Uncle Sanjay brings me a pair of denim overalls and two T-shirts with "Island Lover" written across the front. And a lime green sweater. And a set of pajamas with pictures of whales on them. And thick, striped socks, and underwear and one pair of rubbery shoes. My uncle doesn't have a clue about clothes, but I don't want to hurt his feelings. After all, he's trying.

Chapter Four
MORNING MAKEOVER

"**R**ise and shine, my dear niece!" Uncle Sanjay stands in my bedroom doorway in yellow pajamas. His hair sticks out like the many spikes of a cactus plant.

"What? Where am I? What time is it?" I open my eyes. Oh, yes. I'm in the closet that Uncle Sanjay calls his guest bedroom, in his cabin in the woods, nine blocks from Witless Cove, population 812.

"Here we wake with the sun and sleep with the moon."

Stu is lying on top of me, letting out farts and pedaling his feet in his sleep.

I look up at the ceiling to see a giant spider hanging from a cobweb. I tumble out of bed, screaming. "*Spider! Right there!* Big as a Volkswagen!"

Uncle Sanjay reaches out and grabs the spider in the palm of his hand. "Oh, that little thing. She needs to be in the forest." He carries the spider outside. Through the window, I watch him walk across the grass in his slippers and drop the spider at the edge of the woods.

Back inside, he says, "When we see those spiders, we don't panic. We take them outside. They perform a great service, eating mosquitoes and other pesky insects such as aphids, for example."

I press my hand to my chest. "I almost had a heart attack." But I'm mad at myself. I shouldn't be afraid of a few hairy little legs if I'm going to be a veterinarian.

Uncle Sanjay pulls up the blinds all the way, letting in a burst of bright sunlight. "I'll make us some tea and breakfast, shall I? We leave for the clinic in half an hour."

"Half an hour? But I have nothing to wear."

My mucky clothes are piled like a volcano on top of Uncle Sanjay's washing machine in his laundry room. I left my suitcase lying on the floor, the two halves broken.

"What about your island gear?" His face falls, so I force a smile.

"Right! How could I forget?" I have to wear the denim overalls from the Trading Post, an Island Lover T-shirt, and the lime green sweater. I wish I could go in disguise—a wig and sunglasses. At least I still have my own shoes. I tie my hair back with a slightly soggy green bow to match the sweater.

In the kitchen, we're having huckleberry jam, toast, and lavender chutney for breakfast. I try everything except the chutney. I'm not ready to eat a flower.

"Would you like some tea with honey?" Uncle Sanjay asks.

"I need sugar." I open the kitchen cabinets. Empty spice bottles are mixed in with the full ones. The empty ones are labeled with place names—Paris, Seattle, Miami. Looneyville, Texas; Whakapapa, New Zealand; and Little Hope, Georgia.

"What are these, Uncle?" I have to take out all the bottles to reach the bag of sugar in the back.

"I like to collect air samples. They're all different. I should've asked you to bring some Los Angeles smog."

"We live in Santa Monica, on the western edge of L.A. We get clean air sometimes, too."

"Not as clean as our island air, I'm sure."

"Maybe not." I separate the air bottles from the spice bottles and put the sugar in another cabinet, with the tea bags. "You don't have any bottles from India."

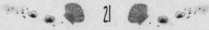 21

Uncle Sanjay sits at the table and spreads lavender chutney on his toast. "Reminds me too much of home. I had a bottle of Kolkata air, but I emptied it. I wish I could go back more often, but India is so far away."

"We go every year, and my grandma visited us last spring. She was always cold. She wore a parka all the time. Dad got teary eyed when she left—"

"I know what it's like to miss family. I became a veterinarian in India a long time ago, nah? But when I got here, my training and experience counted for nothing. People come to America for the opportunities, the great schools, and one can open a private clinic and do very well. But I had to go to veterinary school all over again. I spent years away from my parents. I still miss everyone in India."

"Don't you want to move back there?"

"Sometimes—but this is my home now. My heart will always be in both places. In two countries. But I live here, where I'm needed."

"Don't the animals need you in India, too?" I chew on my toast.

"I've found a place here, where people trust me enough to bring their animals to my clinic. I care for them. They're my island family."

"How did you end up here? I mean, this is the middle of nowhere."

"I followed your ma to America. She was first in the

family to leave her home country." Fingers curled around his teacup, he looks upward and smiles a little, as if remembering a happy moment. "I started in Virginia, then followed her west. I stopped in Seattle and got a job at a clinic there. One day, a lovely woman brought her old German shepherd for a paw massage. I improvised. I don't specialize in dog massage, but I did my best. I couldn't take my eyes off that woman. We fell in love. She was from Nisqually Island, and she wanted to move back here, so I followed her. What we won't do for love. But she was a carefree spirit. When her dog died, she left to travel the world. I'd grown to love the island. So, I stayed." He sighs. "Nothing ever remains the same."

"I'm sorry she left you, Uncle."

"Time heals all wounds, nah? Nisqually Island is a soothing place. I've come to know myself here. I've learned to love the birdsong, the sound of the sea, the cedar trees." He glances at his watch. "Oh no. I was supposed to leave five minutes ago! I lost track of time."

"Are you going like that?" His hair still sticks out on one side and is plastered down on the other.

"Like what?" Uncle Sanjay spreads chutney on another piece of toast.

"Do you have a comb? And your buttons are done up wrong."

He glances down at his white shirt. "So they are."

I do up the buttons the right way. "Do you have an iron for the wrinkles in your shirt?"

"I might have had one many moons ago."

"We'll have to do the best we can without one." I get up, and in a minute I'm back with my brush, comb, and hand mirror from my purse. I make him hold the mirror while I work. My job is harder with Stu's drooling tongue in the way.

When I finish, Uncle Sanjay holds the mirror up at all angles. "My dear niece, I'm handsome!"

"You look perfect." I'm smiling.

"The ladies will come running from all over the islands, nah? You're good at combing my hair."

"I'm good at braiding hair, too. But yours is too short for braids. Plus you're a man."

"You could be very helpful at the clinic with such skills."

A warm tingle spreads through me. "We'd better go. We're already late."

Chapter Five
Lulu

The moment I grab Stu's leash off the wall, he tears back and forth to the front door, claws scrabbling on the hardwood floor. He slips and slides, bumps into the wall, then dashes back, knocking over a plant.

His excitement rubs off on me. I run out the front door, and he yanks me into the cool morning. Uncle Sanjay, carrying a black briefcase, is close behind in his squeaky shoes.

The night left a sliver of moon in the sky, fading as

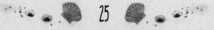 25

the sun rises. In the distance, the ocean twinkles through the trees. Stu squats in the dewy grass, then pees against mailboxes all the way into town. We pass wooden cottages and bright gardens and people out speed walking. Everyone waves, and Uncle Sanjay waves back. His combed hair blows in the breeze, but he still looks handsome.

I trot to keep up with his long strides. "Um, I wonder, could I order another veterinarian kit? My dad gave me some emergency money. I'll also need a white lab coat and vinyl gloves."

Uncle Sanjay grins. "For now, you can borrow a lab coat, and perhaps sometime soon, I'll show you how to use a stethoscope."

"Really? Yay!" I'm skipping along now.

"Working with animals is not only about having equipment. You have to practice, learn, and trust your instincts."

"But you need a stethoscope, don't you? I mean, to listen to a dog's heartbeat, right?"

"Indeed—but the stethoscope is only a tool. You must use your mind, your heart, your steady hands."

"I have steady hands." I hold them up, fingers spread. "They look like yours."

"Yours are much smaller and prettier, and far less hairy." Uncle Sanjay chuckles. "Stu, no!"

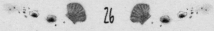 26

Stu is burying his nose in a tipped-over trash can, chomping away on garbage as if the soggy wrappers are a gourmet supper. Uncle Sanjay grabs the leash and drags Stu away from his feast.

Stu instantly forgets the garbage. Now he's sniffing a scent trail in the grass, all the way to Nuthatch Street, a shady lane off Witless Cove Road. At the end of the lane sits Uncle Sanjay's clinic like a gingerbread house in a forest. A bright sign out front reads:

FURRY FRIENDS ANIMAL CLINIC
A HEALING PLACE FOR PETS

Under the sign, a bed of white daisies bloom, surrounded by a ring of small smoothed chunks of frosted glass in a rainbow of colors. I pick up a red piece and hold it up to the light.

"Seaglass," I say.

"From all around these islands. You can find pieces washed up during low tide. Some of these pieces are imported."

"So beautiful." I put the glass back in its place. I want to find treasures like this on the beach.

"Come, we go in the back way, in case clients are waiting to ambush me up front," Uncle Sanjay says. Bumper stickers crisscross the door:

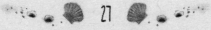

27

I BRAKE FOR VETERINARIANS
I'M A VET, NOT YOUR THERAPIST.
GOT FLEAS? I DO.
ON A DIET? NOPE, TAPEWORMS.

Inside, the air smells of minty antiseptic. The tile floor shines, reflecting the pictures of fluffy pets on bright white walls.

Stu trots down the hall as if he owns the place, and turns left into a room labeled DOC CHATTERJI'S MESSY OF-FICE.

"There's my assistant, Duff!" Uncle Sanjay points down the hall. "I couldn't function without her help."

Duff speeds by as if blown by wind, then stops to stare at Uncle Sanjay. "Doc, you look different today. What is it? New clothes?" Everything about her sticks out—her nose, her spiked blond hair, her shoes, and the pens in the pockets of her blue scrubs.

"My niece combed my hair. She can perform wonders." He pats my back, and I blush.

Duff nods at me and glances at her watch. "You're late. I'll prep for the first appointment." She disappears into a room on the right labeled DOG EXAM.

Uncle Sanjay drags me up front to the reception area. "Announcing my famous niece Poppy Ray! This is my indispensable office manager, Saundra MacLeod." He

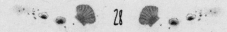 28

speaks so loudly people in the waiting room stare. A cat meows in a carrier.

I'm still blushing. "I'm not famous—"

"She comes all the way from Los Angeles," he says, interrupting me.

Saundra bustles out from behind the counter and envelops me in a hug that smells like a flower shop. Her pink dress squeezes all her curves; her bright red hair is piled on her head in a bun. "Not sure this is the place for a kid your age."

I freeze. What's wrong with my age?

"Please lend her a lab coat," Uncle Sanjay tells Saundra.

She frowns. "But why—"

"And a stethoscope," I say. "And tongue depressors—"

"One thing at a time," Uncle Sanjay says. "Let's start with the lab coat. Saundra, will you do the honors?" He rushes off into the exam room.

Saundra gives me an *I can't believe this* look. "Aren't you jumping the gun, young lady?"

"I'm planning to become a vet." I stand tall.

She looks me up and down, her lips pressed together. "You got a long way to go." But she brings me a lab coat. She chose a large one, maybe on purpose. I have to roll up the sleeves.

Somewhere, a dog barks, and the phones ring, the lines blinking like Christmas lights. "Be careful. Don't go

29

around touching everything," Saundra tells me.

"But—"

"We give clinic tours to schoolkids, but their parents have to sign waivers. If a dog bites a child, the parents promise not to sue us. You're Doc's niece, so we're probably safe, but you'd better not get into trouble anyway, you hear me?"

I nod, but I'm not a *child*. What kind of trouble could I possibly get into?

Saundra dashes behind the counter and picks up the phone. "No, we don't treat farm animals. You need to call Island Vet up in Freetown." She hangs up and frowns at me again. "Young lady, you need to—"

The phone rings. "Uh-huh, we take payments if you've been here before and have established your credit with us." She hangs up. "So, Poppy—oh, wait." She takes another call. "Doc Chatterji does not declaw cats. There are caps you can use on the claws. Sure, you can call up to Freetown, but I don't recommend . . . Hello? Hello?" Saundra hangs up and curses under her breath. "I can't get a minute to myself these days."

The front door squeaks open, and a golden cocker spaniel bursts in and races toward me, wagging her stubby tail. I barely jump aside in time. She scrambles past me and knocks the magazines off the table.

"Good morning, Lulu, Mrs. Lopez!" Saundra breezes

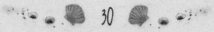

into the waiting room holding Lulu's chart, like a dinner host carrying a fancy menu. She sweeps an arm toward the hall. "Right this way."

Mrs. Lopez tries to grab Lulu, but the little dog prances away, dragging her leash. She looks like her human— same wavy gold hair and droopy eyes. Mrs. Lopez's dress fans out at the bottom, like Lulu's fur. Lulu wags her whole body and wiggles toward me. The moment I pet her, she lets out a stream of pee.

I hop out of the way, nearly losing my balance.

The puddle slowly spreads across the floor.

"Uh-oh," I say. "I didn't mean to—"

"Lulu, not again." Mrs. Lopez scoops up the dog. "She's got a problem with submissive urination. I do apologize."

"Oh, well that explains things," I say, pretending to understand.

Saundra glares at me, as if those two big words, "submissive urination," are my fault. She gives Mrs. Lopez a sweet smile. "No problem—happens all the time." She lets out a fake laugh and turns toward me. "If you want something to do, you can mop it up."

"Me?" I did not plan for this. I'm here to heal the animals, not clean up their pee.

"Mop's in the hall closet." Saundra gives Mrs. Lopez a phony smile. "Now, if you'll come on back..." She heads toward the dog exam room, turning her back on me.

"Sorry I made Lulu pee," I say to Mrs. Lopez as she breezes by with Lulu tucked under her arm.

She touches my shoulder. "Lulu can't help it, sweetheart. She gets excited, especially if she knows that you're excited or nervous—"

"But I'm not nervous—"

"She loves you even if you are. She loves everyone. She's saying hello."

What if humans lived like Lulu, letting loose every time they greeted their friends? Instead of waving at each other on Nisqually Island, they would lift their legs and pee, like Stu did on his way to the clinic. *Oh, hello, George.* Pee. *Howdy, Mary.* Pee. *I love you, Dr. Chatterji.* Pee.

But humans don't love everyone the way Lulu does. At least, I don't. I see a new truth staring from my reflection in the window. I've wanted to be a vet for my whole eleven years of life. But I don't love losing my clothes, or my suitcase, or my veterinarian kit. I don't love being stuck in the middle of nowhere without a cell phone signal. And I don't love Saundra MacLeod.

Chapter Six
GROSS STUFF

"**C**areful you don't step in that pee and track it around," a scratchy voice says behind me. I turn, and I'm staring at a tall, blue-eyed, freckled boy with strawlike hair. He starts cleaning Lulu's pee with quick strokes of a mop. His eyelids are halfway closed, as if the world is so boring that he's falling asleep.

The phones are ringing. Saundra runs back from the exam room. "This is my son, Hawk." She gives him a lovey-dovey *you're my favorite boy* look. She touches his

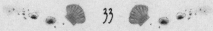

cheek, and he makes a face and steps away from her, looking embarrassed. "He helps us out a couple days a week. This is Poppy Ray, Doc's niece from Los Angeles. She's staying here while her parents are in India. She wants to become a *veterinarian*." She says that last word disbelievingly.

"Hey, Poppy. Nice lab coat." Hawk gives me a flashy grin. "You know any movie stars in L.A.?"

"Know any killer whales?" I ask. My face is hot.

"Saw J-pod this year." His blue eyes are trained on my face. "Out at West Bluff State Park."

I want to ask him what J-pod is, but I pretend I already know. "Well, good for you."

"Come on back," he says. "I'll show you around."

"Don't go touching everything!" Saundra yells after us.

"Can't stop my feet from touching the ground," Hawk mutters, but his mom doesn't hear. He leaves the mop and bucket in the hall and leads me to a room in the rear of the clinic. "Animals stay here if they're boarding, or if they're going to have surgery." He points to cages— small ones on top, big ones along the bottom. A fluffy gray dog trembles in a bottom cage. Bags of pet food line one wall, across from the cages.

"Doc took a tumor off his leg last Friday." Hawk opens the cage to pet the dog. "He stayed over the weekend, goes home today."

I touch the dog's soft fur, and he nudges my hand with his wet nose. His watery eyes gaze up at me as if to say, *Please take me with you.* I want to hug him, but I'm afraid I'll hurt him.

Hawk closes the cage. "Come on. I'll show you some gross stuff."

I follow him down the hall. "I hope you're not going to show me blood and guts. I get queasy."

"And you want to be a vet?"

"Once, when my uncle visited us in L.A., he told me he used to get queasy, too, when he first started out. He was even afraid of needles when he was a kid. But *he* became a vet."

"I can't believe Doc was afraid of needles." Hawk laughs. He points to a hallway branching off to the right. "There's the X-ray room, two surgery suites, an employee lounge. We have a laundry room for washing towels and lab coats. People are in and outta here all the time. Deliveries, lab transport, Doc's relief vet. Come on, this way." He leads me into a room marked PHARMACY. The faint smell of medicine hangs in the air. A white countertop runs along the wall, cabinets above and below.

Hawk opens a cabinet and shoves a jar in my face. Two spongy tan globes the size of golf balls, covered in thin skin, float inside. A stem sticks out of each one.

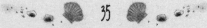 35

Maybe these are miniature deformed brains—the kind crazy scientists like Dr. Frankenstein keep in their laboratories. "What are those things? I hope they're not—"

"When a dog gets neutered, Doc cuts off its testicles. These are dog balls."

My breakfast bubbles up in my stomach. So Uncle Sanjay collects way more than air. "Why does he keep them in a jar?"

"For scientific purposes. I took them to school. Everyone thought it was cool."

"You're trying to gross me out." Speckles dance around in my vision.

"Yeah, and it worked." He shows me another jar, full of thin white strands floating in fluid. "These are round-worms."

"Eeeewwww." I press my hand to the countertop to keep from fainting.

"And these are maggots, fly larvae." He shows me puffed white worms. "A dog came in with open, rotting sores. Maggots grew in them, but Doc cleaned out the wounds. The dog lived. He's fine now, but he almost died. This is what'll happen to you when you're dead. The maggots will eat you—"

"Stop!" The blood drains from my face.

"Hey, you okay?" Hawk grabs my arm and pulls me

toward a chair. "Come here and sit down. Put your head between your knees, like that. Keeps the blood flowing to your brain. I'll be right back."

I follow his orders. Slowly, the pins and needles disappear from the insides of my eyelids.

Hawk brings me a glass of water. "You got a weak stomach, huh?"

I sip the water and take deep breaths. "I'm okay, a little light-headed." My cottony brain slowly clears.

"My mom thinks you're too young to hang out here." Hawk picks at his fingernails. They're short, bitten down.

I glare at him. "I am not too young. I'm eleven. How old are you?"

"Thirteen, old enough to handle this stuff. You were gonna faint."

"I was not."

"Maybe you should go home. Go hang out on the beach."

"I'm not going anywhere. I can be helpful here."

"Oh yeah?" Hawk leans back against the counter. "What are you gonna do, Poppy? Say 'Eewww, gross,' whenever you see a worm or a dog testicle?"

My throat tightens. I glance at the walls, at the pictures of dogs and cats. In one photograph, a smiling blond lady is brushing a collie. I think of the spiffy job I did on

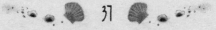

Uncle Sanjay's hair this morning. "I'm a great stylist. I can brush a knot out of any hair."

Hawk's eyebrows rise. "Oh yeah? We got a tangled dog coming in. Name is Shopsy. Bet you can't work your magic on him."

"Bet I can."

chapter Seven
A TANGLED RUG

In the dog exam room, a rug is lying on the table. A tangled rug that rises and falls as if it is breathing. A doughy lady stands in the corner, wheezing. She is wearing a flowery bedsheet that has accidentally become a dress.

Hawk stands in the doorway behind me. I glance at him, and he gives me a look that says, *I bet you can't do it.*

I step farther into the room.

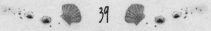

"Hawk, clean up in the hall!" Saundra calls. Another dog must've peed. Hawk disappears, closing the door.

Uncle Sanjay comes in and pats the lady's arm. "Good morning, Doris. We haven't seen you in several weeks."

Doris parts the strands of carpet and points to a red patch. "I don't know if it's an allergy or what."

"Might be an infection. We'll have to shave off some of this hair to get a better look at his skin. You can wait up front. Come, my dear niece." Uncle Sanjay picks up the rug and tucks it under his arm.

Duff is waiting for us in the treatment room with an electric razor in her hand. "What took you so long? Poppy, help me hold Shopsy."

I try to hold the stinky rug, but he squirms.

"He knows you're nervous," Duff says. "Here, let me." She keeps Shopsy from moving while Uncle Sanjay starts to shave off the hair. Underneath, a huge patch of red skin appears, covered in raised red dots.

My skin begins to itch, too.

"Looks like an infection," Uncle Sanjay says. "Let's check the ears." He parts the rug and an ear magically appears. He dips a long cotton swab into the ear and extracts a wad of crusty brown gunk. "See, Poppy? We take a sample, and then we check it for bacteria."

My stomach churns, but I keep a brave face.

Uncle Sanjay peers into the ear. "Duff, better do the cytology."

Duff smears the swab on a slide and puts it under a microscope. "Yeast and bacteria. Take a look, Poppy." She motions me over. "The yeast looks like a boot print."

I press my eye to the lens. Sure enough, miniature blue boot prints march across a field of scattered tubes. "Whoa," I say.

"The other shapes are the bacteria. They're like cylinders."

"Like a whole other planet." I gaze into a world of tiny boot prints and swirls and flakes.

"We need prescriptions for him. Come on."

In the pharmacy room, Duff gathers special shampoo, antibiotic spray, and antibiotic pills.

"That's a lot of medicine for a carpet," I say.

"He needs it." In the treatment room, Shopsy is still lying on the table. Uncle Sanjay leaves to answer a phone call.

"Poor little guy," Duff says. "He looks funny with one shaved spot. He needs a good brushing."

I pick up a comb from the counter. The metal glints in my hand. If I can comb Uncle Sanjay's hair and make him look handsome, I can make a dog beautiful, too.

"Be careful with that," Duff says.

My fingers tremble, and suddenly, Shopsy looks small

and fragile, a breakable dog. He's tangled all over, and I can't see his face. What if I accidentally comb his nose, or his eye, or his itchy ear? Or a sore spot on his red skin? I can't ask him, *Does this hurt?*

"Here, let me do that." Duff reaches for the comb.

"No, I'm good." I take a deep breath and try to work the comb through the knot of hair on Shopsy's neck, but the teeth get stuck.

I'm starting to sweat.

Shopsy fidgets on the table.

"Let me help." Duff holds him, but I can't get the comb to move; it's stuck in his hair. He shakes his head and growls. I pull harder on the comb, and Shopsy yelps.

I let go of the comb and step back. "I hurt him."

"You need practice," Duff says gently. "Here, let me."

I step away. Shopsy whines and trembles.

"Hang in there, little guy." Duff grabs a pair of electric clippers. "Hold still."

I back toward the door. The clinic noises swirl around me; people race by. The phone rings, and a dog barks. I hear Doris's muffled voice from the hallway. "Was that my Shopsy crying? What are they doing to him back there?"

My throat closes.

Saundra's strong, reassuring voice: "Why don't I check

on him for you?" Her footsteps clop down the hall. She pokes her head in the door and glares at me. "What's going on in here?"

"All under control," Duff says without looking up. "Tell Doris five minutes."

"Fine." Saundra's angry gaze pierces a hole in my forehead. Then she clops back down the hall, and I hear her speaking in a low voice to Doris.

Duff starts to trim the knot with the clippers. She works slowly, a little at a time. "I learned to do this using scissors, way back when," she tells me. "You can accidentally cut a dog and not even know it. Sometimes they don't even feel it. You notice when you see the blood."

I feel woozy even *thinking* about blood. "What do you do, stitch it up?"

"If the cut is big, but first you clean it and apply pressure to stop the bleeding. But we don't use scissors anymore. We use clippers. They're safer." She manages to talk while holding Shopsy with one hand and working with the other. The comb is still stuck in his hair, but soon the clump of fur is no longer attached to the dog. A big bald spot appears on his neck.

"Well, that takes care of that." Duff twists and pulls at the comb until it slips free of the hair; then she throws the clump into the garbage.

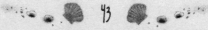

"How did you do that?" I ask. I wanted to make Shopsy beautiful, but I couldn't.

Duff grins at me. Her top front teeth stick out a little. "You gotta feel for the knots. You can't just yank the comb through. You gotta pay attention, and practice. Eventually, you become an artiste."

Chapter Eight
DOG AFTERNOON

Shopsy goes home with big patches of hair shaved off, as if a killer razor attacked him. Doris shouts, "Oh my Shopsy!" and "I'm never bringing him back here again!"

"This is all my fault," I tell Uncle Sanjay in the treatment room.

He spritzes cleanser on the table. "No it's not. Doris doesn't take care of Shopsy the way she should. Look what happens."

"But if the comb hadn't gotten stuck—"

"Shopsy's a matted dog with a nasty skin infection. Perhaps you should try brushing a healthy dog."

Duff has come in, carrying a chart. "Maybe Daffodil. She's a golden retriever. Owner's leaving her here to be groomed later on. We only do the basic stuff. You know—brushing."

"Daffodil, yes! A very sweet dog," Uncle Sanjay says.

Hope sparks inside me again. "I can do more than brushing. I'm good at styling."

Duff grins. "Well, there you go."

But Saundra keeps closing doors in my face—the door to the surgery suite, the door to the exam rooms, the door to the pharmacy room. She smiles at everyone except me. Whenever she breezes past, she screws up her face, like the clinic is a big sugar candy and I'm the only sour drop. "Doris is probably going to take Shopsy up to Freetown from now on," she mutters, turning her back to me.

"I'm sorry," I say. "Shopsy had knots."

She doesn't reply, just keeps answering phones. I peek at a litter of fluffy kittens here for their vaccinations. The needles look scary and sharp, but the kittens don't let out a peep.

A pug puppy comes in for an exam, and a fat corgi with short legs needs to lose half his weight. Uncle Sanjay

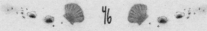

keeps checking on me. He doesn't want me to see anything else gross.

"You can help me in the kennel room," Hawk says, handing me the mop. While he scrubs the empty cages with disinfectant, I clean the floor.

"I didn't realize the place could get so dirty." I wipe sweat from my forehead.

Hawk straightens a few cases of canned cat food. "What did you expect? We treat animals. They have fur. They pee, they poo, they bleed when they're wounded, and sometimes they throw up. Haven't you ever had a pet?"

I lean on the mop and shake my head. The truth comes out. Hawk looks at me, clearly surprised. "Never? Not even one? And you want to be a vet?"

I blush. "So sue me. My mom's allergic to anything with fur."

"That bites. Couldn't you have, like, a turtle or a snake?"

"I don't like the idea of keeping them in glass terrariums. Once, when Uncle Sanjay visited us, we heard about a pet chimpanzee that tore off a woman's face. Uncle Sanjay said wild animals are meant to live in the wild. That goes for snakes and turtles, too."

"Okay, you could get a hamster. I had a hamster once."

"They have fur."

"You could have fish. Fish are cool."

"My dad gave me a goldfish when I was four, but after a few days, it died. I don't know why. I was so sad, I never wanted to have another fish. Maybe that's partly why I want to be a vet. I want to help the fish, too."

"I can just picture it: Poppy Ray, Goldfish Veterinarian. If you want to save the fish, you'll have to learn to scuba dive." Hawk grins at me.

"I'm up for it." I grin back at him. "But I'm going to focus on dogs and cats, mainly."

"You could have a hairless dog, like maybe a Mexican Hairless. Or a sphynx. That's a hairless cat."

"My mom is also allergic to the saliva. Besides, she's afraid of having another allergic reaction. Once, I . . ." I look at the floor. My stomach twists when I remember.

"Once you what?" Hawk steps closer. "You have to tell me."

I sigh. "Okay. Once, when I was seven, I found a fluffy Pomeranian wandering down the street. I smuggled him into my bedroom closet. I wanted a pet so badly."

Hawk's mouth drops open. "You did not."

"I did, but I couldn't keep him quiet. My mom came in, and she had a terrible allergic reaction. She got a rash, and she sneezed up a storm."

"Whoa. I bet you got in big trouble."

"I had to scrub my room, and all the floors, and we washed everything in the house. My dad found the dog's

owner, a lady who lives at the end of our street. I felt really guilty."

"Hey, we all make mistakes." Hawk sprays cleanser on the window and wipes it clean.

Duff pops her head in, her face shiny with sweat. She wipes her forehead. "Hawk, Poppy, come on! Sheesh, this must be puppy day. Things happen this way sometimes. Everything hits at once. You're not going to believe this. We have *two* litters at the same time. One litter is in the dog exam room. But come to the treatment room first. Hurry!"

My heart skips, and Hawk raises his eyebrows at me as we follow Duff down the hall. The treatment room is a sea of puppies, ten in all. They're not small and fluffy. Each puppy is the size of Lulu, a full-grown cocker spaniel, but these are short-haired white dogs with black splotches, gigantic paws, and knobby legs. They totter around carefully, with their legs spread out, trying to keep their balance on the slippery tile floor. They're timid, trembling a little. Their owner, a tall woman with a long face and straight hair, tries to herd them onto a blue carpet. I recognize the paisley pattern—Uncle Sanjay's office rug.

"What a splendid idea to bring in the carpet," the lady says in a strong English accent. "Come, my babies, off the floor. Oh, perhaps they're too nervous." The puppies slide around, trying to avoid the mat.

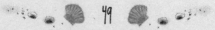

"It's all right," Uncle Sanjay says. "Let them go where they want."

"They look like newborn colts, don't they?" Duff holds a puppy while Uncle Sanjay kneels to examine the paws.

"Great Danes!" Hawk says. He pets the puppies and they wag their tails.

"Thirty pounds each," Uncle Sanjay says. "Healthy specimens. Poppy, Hawk, do you want to help hold them? Gently."

Duff huffs as she lifts a puppy into her arms. "They're only eleven weeks old."

"Only eleven weeks?" I can't believe it.

"They'll grow to over a hundred pounds each," Duff says.

I pet the puppy's soft head. "His face is so big!"

The long-faced lady rushes over and kisses the puppy's nose. "This is Sleepy. His eyelids droop. I named the pups after the seven dwarves but I had to make up three more names. Wakeful, Hoppy, and Dizzy."

Hawk smiles, and his lips twitch, like he's trying not to laugh. I help him hold the puppies, one by one, so Uncle Sanjay can listen to their hearts and examine them. "Duff weighed them when they came in," he says to me. "We always weigh the animals first. She takes their temperatures as well."

"That was fun," Duff says, rolling her eyes.

"We didn't take all the temperatures this time," Uncle Sanjay goes on. "A few of the puppies are too nervous, so we'll wait until their next visit. They'll be back for more vaccinations in a couple of weeks."

After the Great Dane puppies leave, we all gather in the dog exam room to help with the other litter of puppies. Nine Alaskan malamutes. "Seven weeks old," Uncle Sanjay whispers. "About ten pounds each."

They're much smaller and fluffier, and they're not nervous. They're asleep on the floor.

All of them.

A few are lying on top of each other in a heap, and a few are stretched out on their backs, snoring.

Their owner—a man with soft, fluffy hair and sleepy eyes—sits on the bench, his thick hands clasped in his lap. "They're pooped out," he whispers. "My wife and daughter played with them all morning, and the drive tired them out, too."

Uncle Sanjay lifts a dozing puppy. "They're still young. They sleep a lot."

Duff holds a fluffball in her arms. "Poppy, do you want to take this one? It's a girl."

When I cradle the pup, I'm so happy I can hardly breathe. "She's so warm and heavy," I whisper. "She's not even waking up."

Duff carries a sleeping puppy to the scale to weigh

him. "Days like this, I love my job," she says.

I'm going to love my job, too, if I get to hold fuzzy puppies all the time.

Saundra pops her head in the door. "Daffodil's here," she says. She frowns at me.

Duff motions for me to follow her to the treatment room, where a magnificent golden dog trots back and forth. Her long, wavy hair flutters, and her tail wags like a flag. Daffodil is like the royal, celebrity version of Stu.

"Here, go for it. Do your styling magic." Duff holds the dog while I run the comb through her hair—not a single knot, just a few kinks. When I'm finished, Daffodil looks spiffy.

Saundra calls from up front, "Daffodil's owner is back to pick her up. Can you walk her up front, please? And, Duff, you have a call on line two."

"Hang on a sec." Duff steps into the hall to answer the phone. I pull the bow from my hair and tie it on top of Daffodil's head. She looks beautiful now. I grab her leash and trot her into the hall, past Duff, who's waving her arms at me. I wave back, and when Daffodil and I make our grand entrance in the waiting room, a tall man is standing there in a leather jacket; a red bandanna is around his head, a tattoo on his cheek. He takes one look at the bow on Daffodil's head and bellows, "What have you done to my dog?"

Chapter Nine
THAT SANJAY

I hide in the kennel room. Stu wanders in and sits next to me, as if he knows I'm upset. He rests a paw in my lap.

"I messed up with Daffodil and Shopsy," I tell him, "but I need to keep trying, right?"

He looks into my eyes. Stu might give me wise advice, if only he could talk.

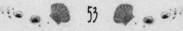

"I have to do more than hold puppies. What if I can't learn to brush a dog?"

Stu's tail thumps on the floor. I pet his ears. "You don't care either way, I know. I wish I could be like you."

On the walk home, he sticks close to me. He doesn't slobber or stop to bury his nose in garbage.

"My dear niece, don't worry," Uncle Sanjay says. "It was your first time at the clinic, nah?"

"Daffodil's owner hates me now. He ripped off the bow." Now I know why Duff was waving her arms in the hall. She was trying to warn me.

"He doesn't hate you. He needs to get in touch with his feminine side." Uncle Sanjay chuckles. We stop to let Stu pee against a mailbox.

"Doris won't bring Shopsy to the clinic ever again."

Uncle Sanjay waves his arm. "Bah. She says that every time."

"Except for the puppies, my first day sucked."

"The days will get better, but sometimes you must endure difficulties first. I thought becoming a veterinarian was going to be all fun and games. I pictured Dr. Dolittle surrounded by talking animals. But real life is messy. We see so many sad cases. Sick pets, old pets, some hit by cars. I do my best, but I can't save all of them. My skills only go so far."

"Mine too. Mine don't go anywhere."

"You'll keep learning. What matters is what you begin to know about yourself."

I'm not sure I've learned anything.

When we get back to the cabin, Uncle Sanjay boils water for tea, and just as the kettle starts to whistle, my parents call. Mom's voice, eight thousand miles away, echoes across the wide ocean. "Poppy, how are you? We're staying with my parents. We've also seen your dad's ma and a few of your aunts and uncles. They send their love. They miss you."

"I miss them, too." I wrap the long telephone cord around my wrist.

"Wish you were here, sweetie. How was your first day with Uncle Sanjay?"

I want to tell her about the worms in jars and my disasters with Shopsy and Daffodil. But I tell her only the good stuff. "Two litters of puppies came in. Nineteen of them! My day was amazing. I'm so glad I came here."

Uncle Sanjay hands me a cup of tea, his eyebrows raised. I give him a woeful smile.

"I'm sneezing just thinking about all that fur," Mom says. "But I'm glad your visit is going so well. Have you heard from Emma and Anna?"

"They don't have cell phones at camp," I say.

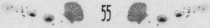

"Are you making new friends on the island?"

"I've only been here one day!"

"Seems we've been away from you forever. Hold on, your grandpa wants to talk to you. Bye for now, sweetie. Love you!"

A moment later, my grandfather's deep, gruff voice comes on the line. "Poppy, why aren't you here with us? Why are you staying with that Sanjay?"

"I miss you, too, Dadu." I've always called him that, the Bengali word for a grandfather on the mother's side of the family. "How are you?"

"My feet are paining, and my heart is weak. If that Sanjay had become a surgeon, he could've taken care of my heart. But he insisted on working with cows and goats—"

"Mostly dogs and cats. He's a great doctor."

My grandfather harrumphs. "Don't get bitten by one of those wild beasts. You don't want to come down with rabies."

"I don't have to worry about that here—"

"Next time, you come to India, nah? Everyone sends their love. Let me speak to that son of mine."

I hand the phone to Uncle Sanjay. He listens, murmurs, and says "yes" a few times. "Give everyone our love," he says. When he hangs up, he's quiet. Then he rubs his forehead. "Ah, family. I miss them."

"Me too." I miss Mom's clinking bangles. I miss Dad calling me Poppykins.

Uncle Sanjay comes over and rests a hand on my shoulder. "Come, let's forget our worries and have a little fun. Would you like to go to a festival? We still have time. The evening is young."

chapter ten
EVERYTHING LAVENDER

At eight o'clock, the sky is still bright, as if it's only late afternoon. Uncle Sanjay drives me through town to a special "surprise" festival. I bring ten dollars in my purse.

"Don't tell your ma and dad that I'm taking you out so late." He winks at me. "We have long days here in July. We're so far north, nah? We have light in the evenings and time to go to the fair."

"Is there a roller coaster? A Ferris wheel?" I grab the

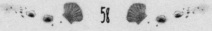

door handle as the truck sputters over bumps. Stu keeps farting. His breath smells like rotting seaweed.

"It's not that kind of fair." Uncle Sanjay adjusts the broken rearview mirror, which tilts downward, giving him a view of Stu's rear end. "No rides and such, but I'm sure you'll enjoy yourself. It's a special annual island festival, happens every July."

"What's there? Is it like the Santa Monica Pier? My friends and I like to ride the carousel. There's a juggler on stilts—"

"You'll see." Uncie Sanjay is driving out of town now, where the hills rise and fall and roll away in bright green and pink and blue. A sweet, perfumy scent rises through the air.

Uncle Sanjay turns down a dirt road and parks in a clearing with about a hundred other cars. Stu leaps around, wagging his tail and whining.

"We have to walk through the woods to the farm area," Uncle Sanjay says.

"We're going to a farm festival?"

The gravel trail goes on through the woods forever. The forest is beautiful, though, with the fading evening sunlight sprinkling down through the leaves, moss creeping through the shade, and flitting sparrows. Stu's happy enough to chase birds, keep his nose to the ground, and sometimes chew on a rock. Stu is always hungry. I bet he

sees the world as food. Tree bark = food. Rocks = food. Dirt = food.

As we walk, we see people strolling in the opposite direction, toward the parking area. Some carry bags; some are licking ice cream cones; and others are carrying fold-up chairs. My heart starts to beat a little faster.

"Sometimes I walk here, when I need to get away," Uncle Sanjay says. "My work can become quite stressful. The forest helps me relax."

"When I get upset, I sit in my closet," I say. "I have a lot of space in there. It's quiet, too. I bring my flashlight and read."

Uncle Sanjay takes my hand. "You and I are alike. We both need a sanctuary."

I never thought of that before, but it's true. From our house on a hill in Santa Monica, I can hear the loud rush of traffic. But in my closet, the sound fades to a murmur.

"Here we are," Uncle Sanjay says.

All of a sudden, the trees come to a dead stop. We're standing at the edge of a crowded field full of white tents. A big sign reads LAVENDER FESTIVAL.

"A *flower* festival?" My mouth drops open.

"Lavender is much more than a flower, my dear niece!" Uncle Sanjay leads me down the first aisle of tents. He keeps Stu close on a leash. We stop at a booth full of lavender soap and lotion and potpourri.

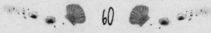

"Come here, honey, and I'll give you a sample." A lady dressed all in pink slaps lotion on my hand, sprays perfume on my cheek. I buy lavender soap for Mom and walk away in a cloud of scent. A bee buzzes by and brushes my hair. Stu's nose works a mile a minute in my direction.

At another booth, I try on a hat made of lavender stalks—and I buy a lavender candle. We even buy lavender dog biscuits for Stu. He inhales them all in one gulp, and he tries to eat my lavender shortbread cookies, too, but Uncle Sanjay stops him.

"These taste . . . purple," I say, but I can't stop eating them. I sample all the lavender foods—jam and jelly and honey mustard and chutney. I buy a jar of chutney for Dad and two bottles of chocolate sauce for Emma and Anna. I can't wait to tell them about the festival, about the man on a stage giving a talk about—you guessed it— lavender. I learn that there are thirty-nine species of lavender plants in the mint family, and that lavender is used to keep moths away, and as medicine and tea, and for healing wounds. There's even lavender ice cream; the flavor is like flower honey.

Uncle Sanjay strides ahead to a booth and leans over to talk to the woman sitting behind the table. She reminds me of a mermaid—white skin with a flush of pink, and long red hair that floats down past her shoulders. She's wearing a necklace made of tiny chunks of green seaglass.

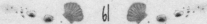

Her eyes are the greenish blue of the sea, and I half expect her legs to be made of fish scales and fins, but her ankles stick out of a gauzy green dress, and she's wearing sandals on her narrow feet.

"Francine and Droopy are looking forward to seeing you tomorrow," she says to Uncle Sanjay. Her voice is soft. She hands him a lavender silk eye pillow.

"Tomorrow is it?" Uncle Sanjay sounds surprised. He turns the lavender pillow over and over in his hands. "Are they all right?"

"Francine has a bit of an eye infection."

"Bulldogs are prone to skin and eye problems." Uncle Sanjay sniffs the eye pillow and puts it gently on the table.

The lady smiles at me. I can't move. I wonder if she's casting a mermaid spell. "Who's this young lady? I see the family resemblance. Is she your daughter, Doc? Are you keeping something from me?"

"This is Poppy, my dear niece visiting from California. My sister's daughter."

"Ah." The lady takes my hand. Her mouth stays open after the "ah," and she squeezes my fingers. "I'm Toni Babinsky. You look worried, Poppy. I can tell when someone is troubled, or uncertain—furry or human."

"I'm perfectly okay." I pull my fingers out of Toni's grip.

She hands me a miniature purple pillow, the size of a

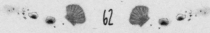

quarter. "Lavender sachet," she says. "In a time of stress, take a whiff. It has a calming effect."

I press my nose to the fabric and breathe in the strong, sweet scent. "Can I keep this? How much is it?"

"No charge. You'll need it."

"Thank you," I say politely. How does she know I'll need it?

chapter eleven
TWO DOGS AND A PSYCHIC

First thing in the morning, I accidentally step in poodle pee and track it around the clinic. Saundra glares at me, but Hawk comes to my rescue and mops the floor. I wash the bottom of my shoe with antiseptic soap.

My second day is just great so far.

Toni Babinsky comes in at ten o'clock. She sits on the bench in the exam room, two dogs at her feet. She's wearing a long blue dress that ripples and shifts in waves, and a matching seaglass necklace. The bulldog, Francine, is snorting and sniffing. Droopy, a skinny brown mutt, cringes in the corner. Francine has a wrinkly face, a stocky body, and two long bottom teeth that stick out. She flops onto her back, right on my foot, her stubby tail thumping.

Duff comes in and raises her eyebrows at me but doesn't kick me out. "Hello, Toni!" she says cheerily. "What's new since your last visit?"

"Francine has gained weight, I'm afraid."

Duff hauls Francine onto the floor scale, but Francine keeps flopping over to be petted.

Toni smiles. "She's a handful, isn't she?"

Francine rolls off the scale, and Duff gets up to write in the chart. Her cheeks are flushed. She puffs from the effort of hauling Francine. "She's good and, uh, solid. I see Droopy came along for the ride again. He's not on the schedule for an exam."

"The two are inseparable." Toni smooths her silky blue dress, which is covered in tiny brown dog hairs. "Wherever Francine goes, Droopy goes. Brother and sister."

They don't look anything alike.

"How's Francine holding up?" Duff asks.

Toni rattles off Francine's problems—eye infection, bad breath. "I wipe down her wrinkles with tissue, but I don't scrub them. Her skin is too sensitive."

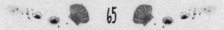 65

Duff scribbles in Francine's chart. "Doc can give you more eyedrops for her."

"He's the best." Toni rummages in her purse, then pouts. "I forgot my wallet. I took it out when I switched purses this morning. . . ."

Duff blushes. "Doc will work it out, like always. He's running behind, but he'll be with you soon." She slips out.

Toni sits back on the bench, crosses her legs, and smiles at me. "I still see trouble, honey. You got your lavender sachet?"

"I left it in my bedroom today. Smells like perfume in there now." I sit beside her, my hands clasped in my lap. "Are you psychic?"

"I rescue animals. I can tell when they're disturbed. Same goes for people. I'm a nurse up at Nisqually Island Retirement Center. I know when the residents are in distress, and I see that you're in distress, too."

"I've always wanted to be a vet like my uncle, but things aren't going too well."

She leans in toward me and lowers her voice. "Doc and I, we're friends. You know what he told me? Things didn't go so well for him at first, either. He's such a caring man. Too bad his father never understood. . . ."

"What do you mean?"

"His dad wanted him to be a surgeon, or an engineer. Veterinarians are not well respected in India. Your uncle told me so. That's partly why he came here. His father wouldn't talk to him for a while after he started veterinary school—"

"But Uncle Sanjay didn't tell me all this."

"He doesn't want to tarnish your dream. He had many bumps in the road to becoming an animal doctor."

I want to hug Uncle Sanjay. I'm glad he didn't listen to his father. Now I understand what Dadu meant when he said, *If that Sanjay had become a surgeon, he could've taken care of my heart.* "My parents say I can be anything I want."

"Good thing, but even here, doctors like your uncle don't always get the respect they deserve. Your uncle is a very determined man. He forges ahead because he loves what he does. He had to learn about many species in school, not just one. Dogs, cats, horses, cows, pigs—"

"I want to learn about all those species, too."

"Maybe you will, honey. The universe has a plan for you."

"A plan? Like what?"

"I won't know unless I read your soul. I dabble in the spiritual arts. I could do a reading for you tonight, around seven?"

I nod, my heart beating faster. "How do you do a reading?"

She laughs. "First, I meditate and communicate with

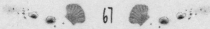

the spirits. I receive information clairvoyantly, in the form of visions. Clairsentiently, through feelings, and clairaudiently, through sounds. Clairolfactorily, through smells."

"How did you learn all that?"

"I started when I was twelve, after I shoplifted a pack of tarot cards."

"You stole?" My mouth drops open.

Francine snorts, and Toni nervously brushes the dog hairs off her dress. "Not my proudest moment, but I wasn't allowed to have those cards. My parents thought I was possessed by the devil. I was actually channeling spirits of long-dead loved ones and transcendent beings."

Uncle Sanjay comes in. "Sorry for the delay." He flips through Francine's chart. "How's my favorite bulldog today?"

Even though my uncle looks like he just walked past a fan, even though his hair sticks out wildly and he needs to clean his glasses, he looks strong and wise. He didn't give up, no matter what anyone said. He traveled halfway across the world to follow his dream.

chapter twelve
THE READING

"**Y**ou're going where?" Dad says on the phone. The line is full of static.

"To see a psychic!" I shout with my mouth full. We're in the middle of supper. I'm scarfing down my curried tofu. It's nearly six-thirty.

"What's that uncle of yours up to?" Dad sounds worried.

"Nothing. I'm just getting a reading."

Mom comes on the phone. "We saw some cousins

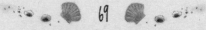

69

yesterday. Your auntie makes the best *mishti doi*. Such smooth, sweet yogurt. Delicious. Dad couldn't stop eating. I'll try to make some when we get home. Are you all right?"

My mouth waters for *mishti doi*. "Everything's great. I'm going to see a psychic who hears the universe clairaudiently."

"Clair-what? Poppy, what's going on there?"

"Don't worry about me. I'm about to discover my inner self."

"Your what?"

"Stu! No!" Stu is trying to steal tofu off my plate. "The universe has a plan for me."

Mom sighs. "Put Uncle Sanjay on, will you?"

I hand him the phone. He nods, listening, then says, "She's doing all right. Dropped her suitcase. Yes, yes. Long story. Her veterinarian kit was ruined. Clothes needed washing. I bought her some island gear."

I glare at him. Why is he telling her? She'll fly me to India in a minute.

"Yes, yes. Give everyone my love." Uncle Sanjay hangs up.

"You were supposed to tell her I'm having a great time!" I say.

"I know you wanted to tell your parents only the good things yesterday, but they should know the whole truth, the good *and* the bad."

"But I won't get to stay here. Mom will send a plane ticket, and I'll have to leave—"

"We won't let that happen, nah?" Uncle Sanjay pulls on a sweater. "Come, let's go."

He walks me five long blocks to a yellow bungalow with flower-filled window boxes. The small garden is lined with rows of bright flowers. Two giant cedar trees stand on each side of the brick path to the porch.

A sign on the front door reads:

TONI BABINSKY, RN
FOSTER CARE FOR CATS AND DOGS,
INTUITIVE CONSULTANT
550 SITKA SPRUCE ROAD

"Intuitive, my foot," Uncle Sanjay mutters under his breath. He rings the bell. Stu prances around, his tongue hanging out.

Toni answers the door in a flowing green robe, the dogs barking by her feet. "Doc! And Poppy! I'm so delighted you could make it. Why don't you come in?"

Stu trots past Francine and right on inside. Francine wags her stubby tail, but Stu ignores her.

Toni stands back to let us pass, but Uncle Sanjay looks up at the darkening sky and shoves his hands into his pants pockets. "I've got lots of catching up to do,

1

patient charts to write up, that sort of thing."

"You'll be missing all the fun," Toni says.

"I'll come back for Poppy in half an hour, all right?"

"You're leaving me here?" I step backward and give him a *don't leave me here alone* look. He's supposed to come in with me.

"I promise I'll be back," Uncle Sanjay says.

"Come on in, honey." Toni smiles.

Okay. I take a deep breath and step inside.

Her house smells of incense and potpourri. I try not to sneeze, for fear of disturbing all the crystals and beaded curtains. Rocks and chunks of seaglass decorate the windowsills. Francine snorts and flops over to be petted, and Droopy cringes under a table but wags his tail when he sees Stu. Stu and Francine chase each other around the house. Well, Stu chases. Francine waddles.

A black cat is curled up at the top of a kitty condo, and a white one perches on the windowsill, watching the birds outside and flicking its tail.

"Those two are Hansel and Gretel," Toni says, leading me through the living room to a covered back porch overflowing with ferns. "Found them in the grocery store parking lot, in the Dumpster."

"In the garbage? Why would anyone do that?"

She shrugs. "What can I do? The universe put those kittens in my path. I had to help them. Sit down." She

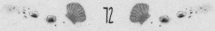

12

waves her arm toward a round wood table. "I'm making tea. Healing relaxing herbal blend?"

"Any kind is fine." I sit at the table, pushing hanging ferns out of the way.

Toni bustles into the kitchen and shouts while she clinks cups. "Doc's a good man, lets me bring in the animals at a discount. He knows I'm strapped."

He lets her bring them in for *free*.

Toni bustles back out with two cups of tea and a teapot shaped like an elephant. She sits across from me at the table and takes my hands in hers. "Now, don't talk. Let me read your spirit. Some readings don't turn out properly because, well, the person won't shut up. If you stay quiet, you'll learn."

I nod and sip the tea, a burst of lavender flavor.

"I'm tuning in to your energy. Repeat after me these affirmations: I am love."

"I am love."

"I am divine."

"I am divine."

"From this place of clarity, breathe in strength and power, energy from Mother Earth."

I breathe in the scent of Stu's farts.

"Breathe out love and feel your heart working." Her eyelashes flutter, and she makes a deep growling sound in her chest.

73

Droopy dashes off down the hall, and I wonder if this is why he has been so jumpy, because of Toni's growling.

"You're troubled. You don't have faith in yourself. You must get in touch with the hidden you."

"The hidden me?"

"You must get in touch with your inner strength. You have to meditate."

"Meditate? How?"

"Hmmm, let's see. You need a special meditation stone, one that you discover on your own, in the natural world."

I stare at her necklace. "What about . . . seaglass?"

Her eyes brighten. "Ah, yes! Beach glass, mermaid's tears, lucky tears—glass that washes up on the beach, smoothed by sand and sea. The best seaglass is round, clear blue, and very rare, but you can settle for amber or green."

"What do I do with it?"

"Every morning, sit cross-legged and breathe deeply. Gaze into the seaglass, then close your eyes and be still and silent, preferably with a friend to help you. Let go and relax."

"And then what?"

"Quiet, patience. Open your mind. The seaglass provides a window to your inner self." She takes a deep breath, and glances at her watch. "Oops, well, that's all

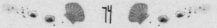 74

for today. I have to feed the fur babies and give them their meds."

"My uncle has seaglass in the daisy garden at his clinic."

"You must discover your own specimen—pristine, untouched."

I know just where I'll search in the morning. Witless Cove Beach, here I come.

Chapter Thirteen
HIT AND RUN

Fifteen minutes later, when Uncle Sanjay, Stu, and I are back at the cabin, the telephone rings. The sound echoes through the house. Uncle Sanjay answers and listens. "Slow down, Harv," he says in his *I'm hypnotizing you into calmness* voice. "What happened? Yes? Oh no!" He nods, shakes his head. "Bring Bremolo in right away."

Uncle Sanjay hangs up, makes another quick call. "Duff, meet me at the clinic. Now." He runs out to the truck. I dash after him, carrying his keys. He's patting his pockets, looking for them. Stu lopes out after us and jumps around, waiting to get into the truck.

"Stu, you stay," Uncle Sanjay says, pointing at the door.

Stu's tail instantly drops between his legs.

"I want to come with you," I say.

"Hurry, then—put Stu in the house. Just this time, so he doesn't get in the way."

Stu is not happy to be locked inside. I hope he'll be okay. Uncle Sanjay is quiet and tense during the drive. The sun is setting, sending fingers of red across a bright blue sky. The air hangs thick and still.

"What's happening?" I ask.

"Bremolo was hit by a car. Usually, I send people to the emergency clinic up in Freetown after hours, but Harvey and Bremolo are my friends, and Harvey sounded so desperate."

When we get to the clinic, a round man is standing on the doorstep, carrying a white poodle speckled with blood. The man is shaking, and when we get out of the car, I see he's crying. "He ran right out in the road. I couldn't stop him."

Uncle Sanjay slides the key into the lock and opens the door. I'm shaking, and Harvey is shaking, but Uncle Sanjay is calm, like a lake without wind.

Inside the clinic, he turns on the lights. Then he carries the poodle into the surgery room and shuts the door.

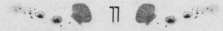

A moment later, Duff rushes in. She looks different without her blue scrubs on—younger and softer in jeans and a T-shirt that says *PET ME*. She hugs the round man. "Harvey, don't worry, we'll take good care of Bremolo. You wait here. You too, Poppy."

Harvey and I are standing in the waiting room. Blood stains his hands; dark red droplets on the ground lead back to the surgery room. My throat tightens.

"The bathroom is that way," I tell him. I point down the hall.

He comes back with clean hands, and I sit beside him.

He speaks in a rough voice full of tears. "I don't let him out on his own, but he likes to chase squirrels. He's not young anymore. He's almost fifteen, that dog, but he can still run. I shouldn't have opened the door."

"It's okay. My uncle will save Bremolo." I want to turn the clock backward and stop Bremolo from dashing into the road.

"The car hit him so hard. He flew through the air. The car took off. Kids! I didn't even a get a license plate. I think they were off-islanders."

For the next fifteen minutes, Harvey keeps talking. I learn every detail of Bremolo's life. I learn what he likes to eat and I hear about the time he mated with a female dachshund, who had tiny poodle-dachshund puppies. I wish I could put on my Superwoman cape and save that

little dog. But I can only sit here, until Uncle Sanjay comes out, pulling the surgical mask off his face. His white coat is splattered with blood. Duff comes out after him, looking at the ground.

I hold my breath for a million years, or maybe only a second, and then Uncle Sanjay says, "He's stable and resting now."

Harvey's shoulders heave, and he breaks into gasping sobs. "Thank you, Doc. Thank you. That dog is my whole life."

"But we couldn't save his left rear leg."

Harvey steps back, blinks, and wipes his eyes. "His leg? How much of his leg?"

I can't breathe. Poor Bremolo.

"We had to amputate above the knee. He'll have a very short stump," Uncle Sanjay says.

I'm shaking all over. "You cut off his leg? No!" My voice falls apart.

"It didn't hurt him," he says gently. "Bremolo is asleep. He'll be all right."

"But he'll wake up and wonder what happened to his leg! He'll be limping forever!"

Harvey smiles through his tears. "But he's alive. That's what matters. My Bremolo's still with us."

"Yes," Uncle Sanjay says. "Duff will stay here with him. You can probably take him home tomorrow. He'll need

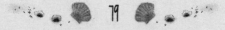

medicine for the pain and to prevent infection."

Duff leads Harvey into the back room to see Bremolo. I can't go back there. I can't look at the poor three-legged dog. I crumple onto a chair in the waiting room.

Uncle Sanjay sits beside me and gives my shoulder a pat. "I had to remove most of the leg, Poppy. The bones were shattered."

My throat closes. I can't speak.

"Bremolo's a lucky dog. The damage could've been much worse. He could've died."

I nod, but a dry lump is growing in my throat.

Harvey and Duff come back up front. Harvey takes a deep breath and pulls out his wallet. His eyes are red and puffy from crying. "How much do I owe you for saving my precious boy?"

Uncle Sanjay waves his arm. "I'll have Saundra send you the bill. Go home and get some sleep. We'll take care of Bremolo."

Harvey nods, wiping another tear from his eye. "I know he's in good hands." Duff walks him out into the parking lot, and I hear him start his car and drive away.

Uncle Sanjay sits next to me, not saying a word, then stands and pulls off his lab coat. "Come, let's go home. It's late. Stu is waiting for us."

On the drive to the cabin, I ask, "What will happen to those people who hit Bremolo? Will they go to jail?"

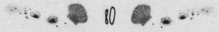

He shrugs. "If Harvey figures out who did it, then he might try to press charges, but it's doubtful."

"So they can hit a dog and go home and not care?" My voice rises.

Uncle Sanjay turns into the driveway and parks, but he doesn't get out. "People drive fast and hit animals every day. Some people keep driving. They don't care." He is silent. "Others stop and try to help. We do what we can."

"Bremolo has to live without a leg!" I'm gripping the door handle, gritting my teeth.

"Harvey will take good care of him. He loves Bremolo very much. They still have each other."

"But he'll have a hard time getting around. Harvey said Bremolo likes to run, and now he won't be able to run."

"Dogs learn. They adapt. Lots of dogs are fine with three legs. They race around as if they still have four legs."

"It's not fair. Poor Bremolo."

"We saved him, Poppy, and the ones we save make it all worthwhile."

When we get out of the car, I hear Stu barking in the house. I hug Uncle Sanjay. The tears are spilling down my cheeks. "We can't let Stu run out in the road, or ever get hit by a car."

"There, there," he says, patting my back. "Not to worry. Stu will be fine. Everything will turn out for the best."

Chapter Fourteen
SEAGLASS

I dream of Bremolo. He stands on his hind leg like a white fluffy circus dog and hops around on crutches.

In the morning, Hawk and I walk Stu on Witless Cove Beach, a few minutes' walk through town. The wide ribbon of sand goes on forever, following the curves of the shoreline. Stu races around, his nose wiggling at piles of kelp, rocks, and driftwood.

I tell Hawk about Bremolo. "One minute, he was happy. The next minute, he got hit, and his leg got amputated."

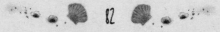

"If anyone can save an animal, Doc can, whatever it takes." Hawk shades his eyes and squints in the sunlight. "But sometimes, there's nothing he can do. I remember a chow dog that got hit by a car. Not a mark on him, but inside, the dog was bleeding to death. We were too late. Doc did his best, but the dog died anyway. The injuries were massive."

"That's so sad." The poor chow. I keep an eye on Stu. He stays close to the waterline, away from the road.

"Another time, a man brought in a golden retriever with a big black tire mark down her back. He didn't see her sleeping on the driveway, backed the car right over her."

I gasp. "Oh no!"

"He said he felt a bump under the tires. He couldn't believe what he'd done. He put her in the car and raced to the clinic. He thought he'd killed her, but she was perfectly fine. Not a scratch on her. No broken bones, nothing."

My mouth drops open. "But how could that happen?"

Hawk shrugs. "Who knows? Maybe it was the way the dog lay on the concrete, or the way the car went over her."

"I guess Bremolo was lucky, too." I reach down and grab a handful of sand, let the grains slip through my fingers. "I hope I get lucky today. I need to find a clear, round piece of seaglass. Toni told me so. I have to stare into the stone and meditate. I'm supposed to search for my inner self."

"Can't you look in the mirror?"

"You're making fun of Toni." I breathe in the smells of salty air and seaweed.

"No I'm not. She gave me a psychic reading once, too. She said I have to be more truthful."

"Are you a liar?"

"Only white lies. The kind that don't matter. Like when my mom colors her hair, she asks how she looks. I always say she looks great, even though her hair looks as red as a fire engine."

"Maybe she wants to know the truth."

"Nah, she just wants me to tell her she's beautiful." He throws a stick, and Stu runs after it, all the way into the water.

"Hey! What are you doing? Stu! Come back!" I chase after him, but I can't run fast in the sand, and I keep tripping over driftwood.

"Don't worry!" Hawk shouts. "Have a little faith, Poppy. He'll come back."

In a moment, Stu trots back with the stick in his mouth. He flops onto his belly and stares at his prize.

"Didn't I tell you?" Hawk throws the stick again, and Stu gallops off into the surf.

"Don't throw it too far." I crouch and sift through a pile of rocks.

"What about this?" Hawk picks up a flat piece of clear glass with part of a paper label still hanging from the corner.

"Not smooth enough yet."

"Probably came from a beer bottle." Hawk pulls a crinkled plastic bag from his pocket and drops the shard of glass inside. "This bag is for garbage and dangerous objects."

We pick up everything from cigarette butts to bottle caps and a couple of empty soda cans. I don't know who could mistake this beach for a garbage dump. Maybe litterbugs need glasses so they can see the true beauty of nature.

We find a few chunks of rough glass, but nothing smooth or round. We also find chunks of pink and black quartz and red and green rocks. Hawk points to round brown spongy shapes embedded in the sand. "Those are anemones. They're alive."

I try to avoid them, picking my way across the boulders. Hawk squats near a small tide pool. "Look, you can see a whole world in there."

The longer I stare, the more I see. Tiny brown crabs scuttle through the water, and red and orange starfish cling to rocks. When I lift a flat stone from the sand, a

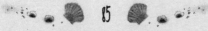

crab scurries away. The beach is full of living treasures hiding in nooks and crannies. I fill my pockets with smooth white clamshells and ridged pink cockleshells, all empty and abandoned by their owners.

We walk a little farther, and that's when I spot something glinting up at me from the sand. A shiny stone, half buried. When I kneel and pick it up, I'm holding a smooth piece of clear green seaglass, the size and shape of a large marble, but flat on the bottom, like a dome. I can see through the glass to an emerald world on the other side.

"I found it!" I yell, jumping to my feet. "I've got my seaglass."

Chapter Fifteen
A LUMP IN A BOTTLE

In the back room, we find Bremolo lying on a pile of blankets in a large kennel. He's on his side, his back left leg a very short stump wrapped in fresh white bandages. He's awake, his watery brown eyes watching us. On the other side of the room, a little Chihuahua is sleeping on a fluffy bed in one of the cages.

"Bremolo looks okay," I whisper to Hawk. "But what is that tube attached to his front leg?" The thin tube leads to a bag of clear liquid hanging from a metal stand outside the cage.

"Intravenous drip. IV. Gives him fluids, a little at a time, so he doesn't get dehydrated."

"You know a lot for a kennel boy."

"I wanna be a technician someday, like Duff."

She pokes her head in the door. "Hey, you two! Bremolo's doing great today, huh? He even ate solid food this morning. Doc wants to keep him here a few more hours, get some more fluids into him. You can pet him for a minute, Poppy. He's a mellow dog. Just don't touch the leg."

I open the kennel and step inside, my heart hopping in my chest. I sit on the blanket next to Bremolo and pet his curly fur. I'm careful not to touch the IV tube. His tail thumps, and tears spring into my eyes. "You're going to be fine," I tell him.

Hawk leans against the bars of the kennel door. "Yeah, you'll be just like new."

"Don't bother Bremolo for too long," Duff says. "He needs to rest." Then she's gone.

I step out of the cage and shut the latch. Bremolo whines softly.

"We'll stay with you," I tell him. "We'll be right here near your cage. Won't we, Hawk? We'll meditate in here."

Hawk rolls his eyes, but he helps me drag dog food bags over near the kennel, to use as chairs. Bremolo is quiet now.

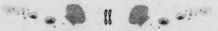

Hawk sits across from me. "So this huge marble is a window into your soul?"

"It's not a marble." I situate the chunk of seaglass on the floor between us. "We have to close our eyes."

"We're not supposed to look into the marble? Aren't we—"

"Hawk, do as I say!"

"Okay, okay. Bossy, bossy."

I shut my eyes, but my lashes flutter. I take deep breaths. I don't remember ever sitting still for so long. One minute feels like an hour. The smells come at me— dog and antiseptic and pet food—and the sounds of the phone ringing, Saundra shouting, the slam of a door, a scared meow, and Hawk's loud breathing.

I open one eye, and he's staring at me. "Are we done yet?" he says. "I gotta pee soon."

"You're not following the rules. You have to keep your eyes closed."

"You opened yours."

"I was checking on you. Let's try again—"

"Wait!" Hawk's eyes pop open wide. "The marble is making me psychic. I heard a doggy thought."

"What thought?"

"From that Chihuahua. He's thinking, *Te quiero, Señorita Poppy Ray!*"

"You have to take this seriously. I need your help. I'm

supposed to meditate with a friend, but I can't concentrate if you're going to mess around."

"Let's try again."

I gaze into the seaglass. Hawk's eyes are closed. Nothing happens.

"Okay, long enough," I say finally. "I'm not seeing anything."

Hawk runs off to the bathroom at top speed. Bremolo and the Chihuahua are both asleep now.

A minute later, Uncle Sanjay pops his head in the door. "Come and see this, my dear niece!" His eyes are bright.

I drop the seaglass into my pocket.

In the treatment room, Duff, Saundra, Hawk, and I gather around Uncle Sanjay. He holds a small clear bottle to the light. There's a tiny lump inside. "Can you believe this? In all my years, I've never seen anything like it."

"You've never seen a lump?" Saundra asks. She's chewing gum and wearing a red and white dress. She looks like a candy cane.

"I thought it was just a kidney-shaped sac," Uncle Sanjay says. "But it's a fetus."

"A fetus!" Saundra gasps.

"Cool," Hawk says.

Duff steps back and blinks. "That little thing? But you were spaying that cat, Dimple. She wasn't pregnant."

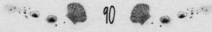 90

"This kitten—this fetus—is mummified," Uncle Sanjay says.

A baby kitten. I curl my fingers around the seaglass.

Uncle Sanjay hands me the bottle. "You're not going to faint, are you?"

I shake my head, although my knees are rubbery. "This doesn't look like a baby," I whisper.

"Remarkable to find the remains still inside the mama cat, intact and not absorbed," Uncle Sanjay says. "This fetus died in its mother's womb, and instead of dissolving, the little body became mummified instead."

I'm holding a bottle with a tiny baby cat inside, in a sac shaped like a kidney bean, maybe an inch long. This kitten did not get a chance to have a life.

Duff peers closely at the bottle. "How is the mama?"

"She's doing fine," Uncle Sanjay says. "She's in recovery."

Hawk doesn't make fun of the lump in the bottle. He doesn't laugh. He looks inside, and then he says, "This baby shouldn't be on display."

Uncle Sanjay takes the bottle from me. "This will be an interesting educational tool. Hawk, you could take it to school—"

"No!" I say. "This kitten needs a memorial service."

Hawk glances at me, then at Uncle Sanjay. "I'm with Poppy. We need to have a funeral."

97

Saundra snorts. "The kitten is gone, honey. She's not going to care. She has vacated the premises. Doc needs to—"

"No no, it's fine." Uncle Sanjay holds up his hands. "Let Hawk and Poppy have a funeral. It's only fitting."

Saundra frowns.

I want to hug Uncle Sanjay.

Duff runs off to an exam room, Uncle Sanjay behind her, and Saundra leaves to answer the phone.

Hawk looks at me. "We need a box," he says. We rummage in the drawers until he finds a large empty matchbox. He wraps the bottle in a tissue and places it inside. Then we go out to the grassy garden behind the hospital. A soft, salty breeze is blowing in from the sea.

We pick a spot near a tall cedar tree and dig a hole. Then we sit cross-legged in the grass and look at each other.

Hawk holds the matchbox over the hole. "We should each say a few words. You first."

I take a deep breath. "Dear Universe, please take this kitten back and let her be born again—"

"Kittens aren't born again."

"How do you know?" I glare at him.

He shrugs, pushes the straw-straight hair out of his eyes. "Okay, you got me. Maybe they are."

"Let her run and play and catch mosquitoes like she's supposed to."

"We're lucky. We don't have many mosquitoes here."

"That's probably because kittens eat them. Aren't you going to say a few words, too?"

"Okay. Dear God, you shouldn't let baby kittens die and turn into mummies before they're born. You need to pay attention. Amen."

"Amen."

He carefully places the box inside the hole, and we bury the kitten and lay a rose over her grave.

Chapter Sixteen
MARMALADE

Every morning for the next three days, I meditate on the seaglass. My parents call every night. They're visiting relatives, and they're meeting with tax lawyers about property they have to sell. Yawn. But when they mention their journeys to historic monuments, or to the bazaar to buy sandalwood, silk, and jewelry, I begin to miss India.

No! I needed to come to Nisqually Island. Animals are my destiny.

The seaglass doesn't show my inner self. It doesn't tell

me how to groom a fragile dog, or how to save baby kittens before they're born, or how to help an old orange cat named Marmalade.

His owner, Mr. Pincus, brings him in just before closing time Saturday afternoon. They're both ancient. Mr. Pincus is all wrinkles that ripple across his face when he smiles. The years pile up in Marmalade's yellow eyes. He's bony and the hair around his mouth is turning white.

Duff weighs Marmalade and takes his temperature. You do not want to know where the thermometer has to go, and it is not pretty. But Marmalade doesn't fidget. When Duff hands him back to Mr. Pincus, he settles down and purrs.

"I've never known a cat to purr at the vet," Duff says, scribbling in Marmalade's chart. "Except when . . . well. How are things coming along with him?" She turns her back to Mr. Pincus.

"He's drinking way more water," Mr. Pincus says in a gravelly voice.

She turns to look at Mr. Pincus. "Shall we check his blood again?" Why is she asking him? He's not a doctor.

"I say let him be," Mr. Pincus says.

Duff nods and walks out. Where is she going? What's wrong with Marmalade? Why didn't she take his blood?

Mr. Pincus holds Marmalade close and rocks him. "My

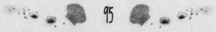 95

wife, she wanted a dog. Never liked cats much. But when
I got Marmalade, she fell in love with him. He followed
her everywhere in the garden, trotted after her when she
planted her bulbs. Flopped next to her when she sun-
bathed. She passed away five years ago. Marmalade was
already twelve years old."

"I'm sorry. . . ."

"We all pass away, eventually. I miss my wife something terrible, but Marmalade helps. He sleeps next to
me. Course, I had to buy pet stairs so he could climb up
on the mattress. He doesn't jump anymore. He's old in
human years, about eighty-five."

Voices murmur outside the door, and then Uncle
Sanjay steps inside. He pets Marmalade, listens to his
heart, checks his ears and eyes, but doesn't lift him onto
the table. He and Mr. Pincus glance at each other and nod
slightly, sharing a silent, secret language. "How can we
help today?" Uncle Sanjay says gently. "For the kidneys,
I can give you—"

"Just the fluids," Mr. Pincus says. "He's drinking up a
storm."

"Of course, whatever will make him comfortable."

What about medicine? What about weighing
Marmalade? What about his kidneys?

"He's still eating," Mr. Pincus says.

"Good, good. Give him anything he wants."

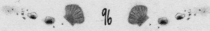

"He still loves chicken and salmon. And corn on the cob. Cantaloupe, too, in small amounts."

"Just stay away from the dangerous foods—grapes, onions, chocolate—"

"I'm very careful," Mr. Pincus says.

Uncle Sanjay prescribes special diets for skin or weight. But now an old, sick cat gets to eat anything he wants?

After Mr. Pincus and Marmalade leave, Duff and I clean the exam room, and Duff says, "That poor old guy. When Marmalade goes, I don't know what he's going to do. He'll be so lonely—"

"When Marmalade goes? Why didn't Uncle Sanjay give him medicine?"

"Marmalade's getting up there in age." Duff scrubs the counter harder.

"But his kidneys—"

"Sometimes, medicine isn't the best way to deal with a problem. Sometimes, you just gotta help the cat feel better." She rushes out to take a phone call, and I stand in the exam room, which suddenly seems smaller and darker than before. The wall clock has stopped at two-forty-five, and on the sink, the bottle of antiseptic soap is empty. A few strands of Marmalade's orange fur still float through the air.

97

chapter Seventeen
BRANDON

I dream of old, skinny Marmalade. He's sitting at the dining table, surrounded by plates of every kind of food—roast chicken, pumpkin pie, curried potatoes, mounds of rice, and filets of salmon. He's wearing a bib, eating whatever he wants. But the more he eats, the smaller he gets. I frantically search for him everywhere, but he has disappeared. I wake up in a sweat. Stu is sitting next to the bed, his tail thumping on the floor. His brown eyes are saying, *Take me for a walk.*

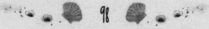

"Oh, Stu." I hug him tightly; then I get dressed and run out to the beach. My dream drifts away, but I can't forget Marmalade, the way he purred in Mr. Pincus's arms.

Monday morning at the clinic, a week after I first arrived, the waiting room is full, the phone is ringing, and a dog is barking in the kennel room.

"Hey, Poppy, you're here!" Hawk pulls me toward the treatment room. "You gotta check out this pit bull. His name is Brandon, after Brandon Roy, who played basketball for the Washington Huskies. Stepped on glass at a construction site."

Inside the treatment room, Uncle Sanjay is fixing the paw while Duff holds Brandon. We watch from the doorway. The dog's back right foot has a big ugly bleeding cut with the skin hanging off. My stomach turns upside down.

Uncle Sanjay is pouring liquid into the wound.

"He's getting the dirt out to prevent infection," Hawk whispers. "He gave Brandon a local anesthetic to numb the area."

Blood drips onto the floor. My legs turn to rubber.

Uncle Sanjay glances up at me. "You all right?"

I am not going to pass out. "I'm fine," I say. The air thickens. I'm having trouble breathing.

"Come in and watch," Uncle Sanjay says.

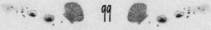

Okay, here I go. We step inside.

Uncle Sanjay smears liquid from a tube onto the flap of skin; then he presses the skin back onto Brandon's foot and holds it there. "This is tissue glue. The army created it for soldiers in the field. If an animal is wounded, apply firm pressure, like this. Very important. If the blood is spurting, it's probably coming from an artery, so you apply pressure above the wound."

The room begins to shrink. Does Uncle Sanjay realize he's making me even queasier?

"If it's a steady flow, the blood is probably from a vein," he goes on. "You need to apply pressure below the cut—"

"Hey, Poppy's looking kind of white," Duff says.

Hawk grins. "Yeah, she's gonna faint." I want to slap him.

Uncle Sanjay looks up again, clearly surprised. "Oh, my dear niece."

Brandon begins to fidget and whine. Duff holds him tighter. She must see my worried face, because she says, "He's mostly upset about being held. Half the time, that's why an animal cries. Not because of pain. Some animals just hate being restrained. You only got so much time until they lose it. Hurry, Doc."

"I've got it." Uncle Sanjay wraps Brandon's foot in a purple and gold bandage. "You wrap from the bottom

 100

up; otherwise you cut off the blood supply to the paw, and the foot swells."

Brandon leaves wearing a cone, called an Elizabethan collar, around his neck, to keep him from chewing the bandage off his foot.

I follow Uncle Sanjay into his office. "How do you do that? How come the blood doesn't bother you?"

"Oh, I've felt sick many times, but after a while, I learned to be calm, inside and out. When you're calm, the animal calms down, too."

"But all the blood—"

"I look past the blood, past the damage. Once, in the late stages of my training, I saw a cow that had its eye gouged out. The eyeball was hanging from the socket. I pictured what I could do to fix what was broken. In that moment, I no longer felt queasy. I believe, in part, we feel faint when we feel helpless. We are stronger when we begin to see the possibilities, to see what we can do."

I'm not yet sure what I can do. I see Shopsy going home covered in patches of bare skin, and I see the blood seeping from Brandon's paw.

But then, right before closing time, Bremolo comes in for a checkup. He trots around the hospital, wagging his tail. Harvey is dressed up in a dinner jacket and pressed slacks, his white hair neatly combed to the side.

"The leg looks good," Uncle Sanjay says.

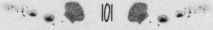

"That old dog is doing so well," Harvey says, grinning. "Runs around the house like he's a puppy again. Doesn't even notice that missing leg."

Saundra pats Bremolo on the head and gives Harvey a fake smile. "You look nice. Going on a date?"

Harvey straightens his jacket and pats his hair. "Dinner at the Witless Cove Pizzeria with Liana Lopez. Taking Bremolo with me. Liana has a dog, too."

I grab a sample bag of dog treats from the kennel room and hand them to Harvey. I'm smiling. "The dog's name is Lulu. Here, this is for Bremolo to take on his date with her."

chapter Eighteen
DUCK ON THE LOOSE

My second Wednesday at the clinic, Duff grabs my sleeve and drags me into an exam room. Inside, Uncle Sanjay is talking to a man who looks like Santa Claus except for his Hawaiian shirt. He brought in a big cardboard box labeled DOLE, with pictures of bananas on the sides.

"Bananas?" I ask.

Uncle Sanjay presses his finger to his lips to shush me.

"I'm sure the poor fella was hit by a car," the man

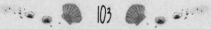

103

whispers. "He was wobbling at the side of the road, on his last legs, God bless his little soul. He let me pick him right up. Good thing I had the box."

Oh no.

Uncle Sanjay ushers me over. He lifts a flap on the box and I peek inside. I'm looking at . . . a duck!

"Is that a geoduck?" I ask in awe, remembering the bumper sticker on the back of Uncle Sanjay's truck: GEO-DUCK FOR STATE BIRD.

Everyone goes quiet. Hawk grins, like he's holding in laughter. Duff stares at me.

"Uh, not exactly," Uncle Sanjay says. "You pronounce it *goo-ey-duck,* and it isn't really a bird. A geoduck is the biggest burrowing clam in the world."

I blush. *A clam?* "Um, so, cool. What kind of duck is this?"

"A male mallard," Uncle Sanjay says.

I've never seen a duck up close. The feathers on his head shimmer in green and gold. A ring of white encircles his neck like a string of pearls.

"What's wrong with him?" I whisper back.

"We don't know yet," Uncle Sanjay says. "Perhaps a shattered wing—perhaps something worse."

The duck isn't moving. I wonder if it's going to die.

"What should we do?" Duff whispers. "We could send him to the wildlife rehab center up in Freetown. . . ."

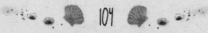

"Not sure he'd survive the drive," Uncle Sanjay says grimly.

Duff runs her fingers through her stiff, sprayed hair. "Ducks mate for life. He has a female waiting for him; you can be sure of that."

My insides melt. A mate. Maybe babies, too. Another animal hit by a car, and the bad guys got away. I'm beginning to hate cars.

Santa scratches his head. "I found him near a big pond. Maybe his mate is still there waiting."

"Let's see what we can see." Uncle Sanjay opens the box. I clutch the seaglass in my pocket.

Uncle Sanjay reaches into the box, but in a flurry of feathers, the duck takes off. Just like that, he spreads his wings and flies out the door and all the way down the hall.

"Cool," Hawk says.

Stu whines. He's probably thinking, Duck = food. But Duff's holding his collar. "Oh, no you don't. Ducks are not dinner for doggies."

The mallard lands at the end of the hall and waddles around, quacking.

"Oh heck!" Santa says. "What do we do now?"

"Quiet," Uncle Sanjay says. "We don't want him to try to fly and hit the window. He could break his neck. We need to walk over there quietly. Grab his wings so he doesn't fly."

"We need a net," Duff whispers.

"Where are we supposed to find a net?" Saundra asks, hands on her hips.

The duck waddles into the women's bathroom. I tiptoe down the hall.

"Where are you going, Poppy?" Hawk whispers, but I'm already at the bathroom door, my heart pounding. I stare at the duck and he stares at me.

"You have to go home to your mate," I whisper to him. "Your babies need you."

The duck toddles over near the toilet, flutters his wings.

"Come on, don't fly away," I whisper.

I have only one chance.

I lunge forward and grab the duck, clamping my hands down over his wings. He's heavy and strong. He tries to flap, but I hold on, making sure not to squeeze too tight. Every molecule inside me knows I can't let go. If I do, he'll fly into the window and die.

"Hold on, Poppy!" Uncle Sanjay rushes over with the box. "Drop him in here."

I release the duck inside the box. My heart is racing. Uncle Sanjay presses down the flaps. "Well done, my dear niece!"

I let out a long breath of relief; my hands are trembling. Everyone pats me on the back, and even Saundra gives me a smile. I'm starting to glow.

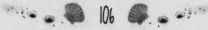

Chapter Nineteen
MOONSHADOW

In the evening, I tell my parents about the mallard duck, geoducks, and everything I can do at the clinic.

"You're an expert, Poppykins," Dad says. "James Herriot has nothing on you."

Early the next morning, after an all-night rain, I help mop the floors and do laundry at the clinic. Around nine o'clock, a black kitten comes in shivering with cold. Her owner, a skinny lady with cropped hair, holds the kitten in a towel. "Thimble climbed a tree and got stuck there

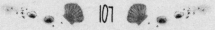

all night. I didn't know she was up there." The lady bursts into tears.

"It's okay, don't worry!" Saundra rushes back to find Uncle Sanjay.

I stand there, looking at the trembling ball of fur in the skinny lady's arms. I try to see the future. I try to see Thimble fluffy and happy and . . . warm.

Uncle Sanjay dashes up to me. "Grab a few towels from the dryer. They should still be warm."

I bring the towels to the cat exam room. Everyone is gathered inside—Hawk, Duff, Saundra, Uncle Sanjay, and the skinny lady.

"We apply them loosely, see?" Uncle Sanjay wraps up the kitten. "Now, Poppy, go with Duff and get a circulating water pad."

I rush after Duff to the pharmacy room, where she grabs a big white heating pad.

Back in the exam room, Uncle Sanjay gently rests the kitten on the heated pad. "The water circulates and distributes the heat evenly," he tells me. "A regular heating pad might burn the kitten. You can keep bringing me warm towels, as well."

Thimble slowly comes back to life and starts mewling softly.

We saved her.

Uncle Sanjay pats me on the back. "You're a good

helper," he says. "Duff, show her a few more basics."

I smile a little. Outside, the sky is clearing after the rain. Dewdrops glisten on the leaves.

"Come on," Duff says. "I'll show you how to weigh the animals."

I practice, and I create my own technique. I hold the cat and step onto the scale, and then I weigh myself without the cat.

POPPY plus CAT equals GIGANTIC WEIGHT

GIGANTIC WEIGHT minus POPPY'S WEIGHT equals CAT WEIGHT

"Hey, not bad," Duff says.

"Poppy, you rock." Hawk pats me on the back.

I'm on a roll.

Uncle Sanjay lets me listen to a cat's heart, which beats more than a hundred times a minute. He shows me the different parts of the stethoscope: earpieces, eartubes, tubing, and the chill ring, which is also called the chestpiece. That's the metal part that presses against the animal's chest.

I even get to help Duff take temperatures. A cat's normal temperature is 101 to 102 degrees Fahrenheit, as high as mine is when I have the flu.

Over the next few days, I learn to brush dogs and cats and cut off knots. My hands are steadier now. I help warm up formula and feed kittens and puppies using an

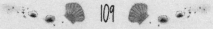

eyedropper. But blood still makes me woozy, and everyone tries to protect me from the gross stuff.

I tell my parents about our second visit to the lavender festival before the tents close down, about my trips to the beach with Stu and Hawk, about the new treasures we find in the sand, the sea lion we see bobbing in the water, waving its flipper. I send postcards to Emma and Anna at their Santa Monica address. They'll be back from camp a few days after I get home.

My second Saturday on the island, when I've been here nearly two weeks, I get to make house calls with Uncle Sanjay.

Stu sulks in the office at the clinic while I help Uncle Sanjay throw bags of prescription cat and dog food into the back of the truck. He secures the tailgate with a rope and brings a giant black duffel bag filled with basic equipment—stethoscope, antibiotics, flea and tick medicine, brushes, syringes, and patient charts—in the front seat.

"I wish I had my first aid kit," I say. I keep the broken box on the bureau in my bedroom, next to the lavender sachet.

"We have everything we need," Uncle Sanjay says. "Some of my clients don't get around much, so I make house calls once every three weeks or so. When I was young, I ran my business out of this very truck."

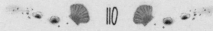

"You did? This rickety old thing?"

"Wasn't rickety back then." He pats the dashboard. "This hump of tin was brand new at one time. Still chugging along. The little truck that could. Even a rusty old heap can still be useful. I made many friends from this truck. It was my office before I got the job in Seattle. Darned difficult it was to find a position at any clinic in those days."

"But why? You're such a great doctor."

He frowns, driving up a windy road on a hillside. "In Virginia, nobody wanted to hire a vet with an Indian accent. They said people wouldn't bring their animals to me."

I twist my hands in my lap. "I wanted to play the princess in *The Princess and the Pea* once, but I had to be the Indian princess that the prince rejected. And I couldn't be Alice in Wonderland."

Uncle Sanjay adjusts the rearview mirror. "So, you understand what I mean. But you mustn't let anything stop you. I became a vet despite the roadblocks. I finally found a job with a Palestinian veterinarian in Seattle. He didn't care about my accent. He had one, too. I met the woman with the German shepherd at his clinic, fell in love, and the rest is history."

He turns down a narrow driveway marked by a sign: NISQUALLY ISLAND RETIREMENT CENTER. I imagined a stuffy

building full of old people who can't walk. But the retirement home, perched on a forested hillside next to the sea, looks like a hotel for celebrities. Inside, the lobby is full of plush chairs and carpets, and it smells like roses.

"Hey, Doc, Poppy!" Toni Babinsky rushes down the hall and hugs us. She looks different as a nurse all dressed in white. I wonder if she gives spiritual readings to the residents. "So glad you could come. Have you been meditating, honey?"

I show her the seaglass, which is still in my pocket. "It's working. I'm helping at the clinic—"

"She saved a duck," Uncle Sanjay says.

Toni whistles. "A duck! This seaglass is an excellent specimen."

Uncle Sanjay's eyebrows rise. "Thanks for the call about Mrs. Morey," he says to Toni. "We'll stop in to see her."

"I'm afraid she's gone off again," Toni says.

Off? I wonder what we're in for.

"Well, thanks for letting me know. Keep me informed, okay?"

"I sure will." Toni blows us each a kiss and bustles away.

Uncle Sanjay and I stop at five luxury apartments, where wrinkly people give us tea and cookies, and Uncle Sanjay checks dogs and cats, leaving food and sometimes flea medicine and antibiotics. We visit mostly ladies,

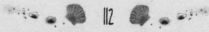 112

some men, and a few married couples. Uncle Sanjay is always friendly and calm, patting people on the back, assuring them that he'll take good care of Fluffy or Fifi or Mitzi or Googoo. I help him, handing him his instruments or holding a light or petting a cat.

"Some of these people need to bring their pets to the clinic," he whispers as we stride down the hall for the last appointment. "I'll talk to Toni about it."

In the last apartment, Mrs. Morey lives alone with a million polished antiques and one gray Persian cat, Moonshadow. Moonshadow Morey. Moonshadow's face looks smashed in, but Uncle Sanjay says Persian cats just look that way—flat-nosed. Moonshadow is mellow and lets Uncle Sanjay examine him and knead his belly.

Mrs. Morey is the nervous one. She keeps pacing, lifting her pearl necklace to her lips. "Oh, poor Moonshadow. So many problems. Dr. Chatterji, I'm so worried he's going to die soon."

Uncle Sanjay pets Moonshadow and checks his ears. "What is he dying of today, Mrs. Morey?"

She paces, gazing out the window. "The lumps, you know. I feed him his favorite foods, and he eats as if there is no tomorrow, perhaps because he realizes there is no tomorrow for him."

"Where are the lumps?" Uncle Sanjay asks.

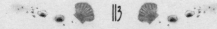 113

She waves an arm behind her, not turning around. "Oh, the usual places. They keep moving. Sometimes on his ears—yes, I felt a lump on his ear this morning, but then it moved to his nose. Maybe it's gone, but it's hiding somewhere; you can be sure of that." She spins around to face us. "You'll find the tumor, won't you?"

Uncle Sanjay nods. "I certainly will."

"And you'll fix it?"

"I have the medicine here." He reaches into his pocket and pulls out a small paper bag, the one he fills with freeze-dried chicken bits to give to the animals as treats.

Mrs. Morey relaxes, folding into an antique armchair. "Oh, Dr. Chatterji, you're a godsend. You'll fix my Moonshadow?"

Uncle Sanjay examines Moonshadow again. "I've found the problem. These should help. My dear niece, will you do the honors?" He hands me the paper bag.

I feed Moonshadow a chicken treat. He gobbles it greedily.

"There," Uncle Sanjay says. "All better."

"But," I say, "the chicken—"

"All done for now," Uncle Sanjay says, and gives me a warning look.

I stare into the paper bag. Can chicken treats heal a tumor?

"Thank the heavens!" Mrs. Morey lifts the pearl

necklace to her lips and kisses it. "What would I do without you?"

"The gods only know," Uncle Sanjay says. He hugs her, and she wipes tears from her eyes.

"How I look forward to your visits, Doctor," she says.

On the way back to the car, I ask him, "What did you do to Moonshadow? What was wrong with him?"

Uncle Sanjay yanks open his door and throws the duffel bag onto the seat. "Nothing wrong with that cat."

I climb into the truck. "Then why did you say . . . ?"

"I told Mrs. Morey what she needed to hear. In her mind, I really was healing Moonshadow with those chicken treats, and he loves them. Every time I see her, Moonshadow has a new disease. Last time he had heart failure. The time before that, a brain tumor."

"But why does she say all those things about him?"

Uncle Sanjay drives down the road and heads into town for our last stop. "Who knows? Sometimes my work is not only about providing the best medical care. It's about providing comfort to those who need it, human and animal alike."

chapter Twenty
SWINGING THE PUPPY

Monday morning, the start of my third week on the island, I wake up and Uncle Sanjay is already gone. Maybe a giant geoduck swallowed him. I shuffle through the house in my slippers, Stu close on my heels. Uncle Sanjay's bed isn't made, but the truck is gone. I find a note next to a cereal box on the kitchen table.

EMERGENCY.
I didn't want to wake you.

Not again.

I glance at the clock on the wall. Seven a.m. I shovel down breakfast and quickly feed Stu. I picture every horrible thing that could've happened. Another dog hit by a car. A duck with a broken neck. Or worse. What could be worse?

I take a deep breath, grab the lavender sachet from the bureau, and take a whiff. The sweet scent calms my brain. I tuck the lavender in my pocket, and Stu and I head out the door. He tugs at the leash all the way into town.

At the clinic, Duff is on the telephone. A lady paces in the waiting room. She's dressed in a long black coat and jewelry made of many colorful rocks, as if she picked them all up from the beach. "Poor Matilda," she says. "I hope she's not in too much pain. I should've called Doc earlier, but I wanted to wait and see if I could handle it myself."

Handle what?

Duff's holding the phone to her ear. She covers the mouthpiece and waves me toward the dog exam room. "Go in there and help Doc," she whispers, then goes back to the phone.

I feel important as I slip into the exam room. Duff sent me in to help Uncle Sanjay. *Me.*

The lights are dim, and a big yellow dog, a fat version

of Stu, is lying on a blanket on the floor, panting. Four little wet rats are squirming around close to her belly. Wait, not rats.

"Whoa!" I say. *"Puppies!"*

Uncle Sanjay shushes me. He's holding a fifth tiny puppy in both hands. He swings his arms up through the air and then down between his legs, then up and down, up and down, in sweeping strokes. "Come on, little guy." He swings the puppy again. "Poppy, this is how we clear fluid from the lungs."

I touch the seaglass in my pocket. I hope the tiny wet rat will live.

"Your turn," Uncle Sanjay says. "She's trying to push out another puppy." He hands me the warm, wet lump.

"But I don't know what to do!"

"Yes you do. First, swing the puppy a few more times." He kneels beside Matilda.

I stand there, frozen, holding the lump in my hands. Time slows, and I hear only my heart pounding. Swinging a puppy isn't the same as grabbing a duck or weighing a cat. Here is a new, fragile life. What if I kill the puppy?

But I can't let the baby die. My arms are moving, swinging up and down, up and down, and then the lump in my hands makes a tiny whimpering sound.

I'm relieved. "He's alive!"

Uncle Sanjay helps Matilda with the last puppy. He grabs a wet rag, wipes the puppy's mouth, and then rubs him vigorously all over. "Here, you try. Stimulates his breathing."

I rub my puppy and then place him next to Matilda, who starts licking her babies. The puppies are squirming and crying and trying to crawl over each other, their eyes still closed.

Matilda's human mom, the rock lady, comes rushing in and crouches down to pet her exhausted dog. "Oh, my brave girl, you did it. Thank you, Doc."

"All six puppies survived," Uncle Sanjay says, beaming.

I'm thinking of the little one that almost didn't make it. I helped him take his first breath. Me, Poppy Ray. I'm beginning to understand what Uncle Sanjay meant when he said, *The ones we save make it all worthwhile.*

chapter twenty-one
GRAINS OF SAND

Wednesday afternoon, when I've been here two and a half weeks, Mr. Pincus brings Marmalade in again. He talks a mile a minute, telling endless stories. "Got into everything when he was a kitten, you know. I didn't call him Marmalade because he was orange. He kept getting into jars of marmalade. Ever known a kitten to eat jam?"

Duff doesn't weigh Marmalade or take his temperature. When she steps out of the exam room, I follow her and tug her sleeve. "You forgot something."

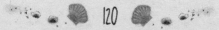

"I didn't forget, kid." She strides into Uncle Sanjay's office and closes the door. I hear her talking to him in a low voice.

Duff and Uncle Sanjay come out of his office, and I follow them back toward the exam room. The whole clinic is quiet.

"Why don't you wait out here?" Duff says, leading me up front. "Isn't the day beautiful? Why don't you go out and enjoy the sun?"

"I want to stay here." I feel like a string pulled tight at both ends. Stu is sitting up front, next to Saundra, resting his head on his paws.

"What's going on?" I ask. But I already know in my bones, in the tips of my toes.

Duff gives me a sad look. Even her spiked hair seems to droop.

I run down the hall and burst into the exam room. Mr. Pincus is sitting on the bench, the bony orange Marmalade in his arms. Uncle Sanjay is standing over Mr. Pincus, resting a hand on his shoulder. My eyes start to water.

"You have to save him," I say. "*We* have to save him."

Uncle Sanjay glances at me, looking startled. "Poppy, you shouldn't be in here—"

"It's all right," Mr. Pincus says in his gravelly voice. "Let her stay. Come here and listen. Put your ear to his fur, young lady."

I lean down and press my ear to Marmalade's soft fur. "He's purring."

"You see, he's content. He's not afraid. Do you want to hold him?"

Uncle Sanjay steps back, tucking a pen into the pocket of his lab coat.

I lift Marmalade and sit beside Mr. Pincus. "He's so fragile," I say. "He's still purring." Marmalade settles into my arms. I'm holding a bag of floppy bones covered in fur, but he's vibrating all over.

"He likes you," Mr. Pincus says. "He knows you care about him." His voice breaks at the end of his sentence, and he presses his hands into his face. His shoulders shake.

Uncle Sanjay rests a hand on his arm again. "We can give you a little time with Marmalade. We don't need to rush."

Mr. Pincus nods, still pressing his hands to his face. "Poppy can stay," he whispers.

"Okay. I'll be back in a few minutes." Uncle Sanjay steps out of the room and shuts the door.

Mr. Pincus fumbles in his bag and pulls out a soft brush. "He loves this. He lets me brush him for hours." He hands me the brush.

My fingers tremble, but I run the brush down Marmalade's back, and he purrs more loudly. His breathing is slow and ragged. He nestles under my armpit. I hold him closer.

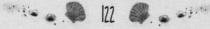

We sit like that, me brushing Marmalade, and Mr. Pincus telling more stories: about how Marmalade caught a mouse in the house once and left it in a shoe as a present. About how he liked to meow at the birds through the window and swipe at the glass. About how he liked to jump onto high shelves and bat Mr. Pincus on the head, with the soft part of his paws so he wouldn't scratch the skin.

"He's had a good long life," Mr. Pincus whispers. "Doc's going to help him cross into the next world, where he'll run around like a kitten again." Tears spill from his eyes. He wipes them away. My chest tightens, and the light flickers and dims. Somewhere outside, a dove lets out a soft *woo-oo-oo-oo* call.

Uncle Sanjay steps back inside. "Are you ready for me now?"

Mr. Pincus nods, swallowing hard. "Thank you, young lady. Marmalade says thank you, too. He will never forget your kindness." Mr. Pincus takes a deep breath and lifts Marmalade from my arms. As I leave the room, I am empty inside. I hold the seaglass up to my eye, but the world isn't clear anymore. The glass is starting to look cloudy. For the first time, I notice black speckles suspended inside. I can't tell what they are—maybe tiny dead insects or grains of sand—but they're trapped in there forever.

Chapter Twenty-two
THE KINDEST THING

I hide in the kennel room. Stu follows and sits next to me quietly, his paw on my knee, as if he's begging me not to be sad. "How do you always know?" I scratch his ears. He watches me, his brown eyes steady, tail between his legs. I hug him and bury my face in his warm, furry neck.

Uncle Sanjay comes in and sits on a pile of cat food bags beside us. "I was wondering where you two were."

"We're in here."

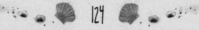

"I'm sorry about Marmalade," he says.

I can't say another word, or my tears will fill the room and we'll all drown.

He rests an arm around my shoulders. "A long time ago, I made a vow to do what I could. To heal. To alleviate suffering. Some people said to me, 'Why are you worrying about the animals when so many people are suffering?' I said, 'The animals are the most forsaken, precisely because everyone says what you say, that their suffering does not matter.' "

Stu flops down on his belly and rests his head on his paws.

"Marmalade mattered," I say, looking out the window. Two mourning doves alight on a tree branch.

"That's what I mean. Suffering is suffering, is it not? No matter what form it takes. Human or animal. We're animals, after all. The human animal. I have always wanted to help the most forsaken ones. I do what I can."

"I wish Marmalade didn't have to get old and die. I wish he could've stayed a kitten forever." The noises in the clinic—a dog barking, doors closing, the telephone ringing—come from a faraway universe.

"Time marches forward and drags us all with it." Uncle Sanjay places his hand on mine. "Without death, life wouldn't seem so precious. We can't have one without the other. Some of us die before our time, while others

 125

get to live a long life. Nobody knows why. We did what was best for Marmalade in his old age, the kindest thing to do."

"Oh, Uncle Sanjay," I say, hugging him. "Why is the kindest thing also the saddest?"

chapter twenty-three
KILLER WHALES

"**U**ncle Sanjay thinks you're very upset," Mom says on the phone in the evening.

"An old cat had to be put to sleep," I tell her. "His name was Marmalade."

"I'm so sorry, sweetie. Pets rarely live as long as we do. Such a shame. Do you want to come to India, see your cousins? We could still get you a ticket. But we don't have much time left here."

"I'll be fine."

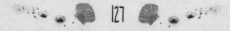

I imagine Mr. Pincus at home in a quiet house, without his kitty meowing at birds or dropping dead mice into his shoes.

The island seems hushed, too, as if the birds are whispering to each other about the cat that went to sleep.

I wish I could forget Marmalade. I wish I could fill the empty spaces. I try to meditate, but the seaglass is cloudy. Every time the door to the clinic opens, my heart beats a little faster, and I hope the next patient will go home alive and well. No more furry friends die over the next few days, but I can't shake the gloominess inside me.

Then, Sunday morning, a week before my parents are supposed to pick me up, I wake to the sound of stomping elephants. The forest is taking over the cabin, and all the wild creatures are moving in.

But it's only Uncle Sanjay rushing around, tidying up and making peanut butter and lavender chutney sandwiches.

"Get dressed, my dear niece. Bring warm clothes."

"Where are we going?"

"It's a secret. We're taking a trip to cheer you up." He grabs a towel and locks himself in the bathroom. I hear the shower running and his off-key singing.

Right after I change into my island overalls, the doorbell rings. Toni Babinsky is standing on the porch, bundled in

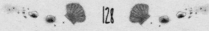

128

a sweater and jeans. She looks pretty with her hair pulled up inside a woolen hat.

Francine and Droopy bounce around in her van, which is parked in the driveway. "Hey, Poppy. How's your meditation coming along?"

I show her the seaglass. I see more speckles today. "A lot has happened. Some things not so good."

"Everything in life is meaningful."

I tuck the seaglass back into my pocket. "Where are we going, anyway?"

"I suggested we go whale watching."

"Whale watching? Really?" I want to be happier than I am.

Hawk comes careering around the corner on his bike, a pack on his back. He parks his bike against the house and trots up onto the porch. "Ready to see some killer whales?"

"Ready as I'll ever be."

"Hey, cheer up." He gives me a playful poke in the ribs. I try to smile.

Uncle Sanjay traipses out and loads two paper bags into the van. "Bring your rain gear. The weather can be unpredictable. I've brought binoculars and water and food."

I grab my blue gum boots and raincoat, which I saved from the stream, and we all get into the van. Stu and the other two dogs clamber around in the back, tails wagging.

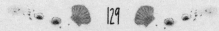

129

They have plenty of room. Toni's van could hold an entire town full of dogs.

I sit beside Hawk in the backseat. Toni drives along the rolling road, past farms and through forests. Now and then, the sea twinkles through the trees.

"How far do we have to go to see the whales?" I ask above the din of the dogs and Indian pop music. Uncle Sanjay is playing a CD with booming drums and high-pitched singing.

"West side of the island," Hawk says. "West Bluff State Park. We pass through Freetown on the way."

Uncle Sanjay chats with Toni about J-pod in the front seat.

"What is J-pod?" I ask Hawk.

"A specific group of orcas. A group is called a pod. Usually, family members travel together. This time of year, you can see their dorsal fins through binoculars. I brought my big ones in my backpack."

The van slows, and we pass through crowded, noisy Freetown, nothing like Witless Cove. Shops are every-where, people spilling out. Concrete sidewalks. Straight new roads. Then the meadows and forests creep in again, taking over.

"How big are the orcas?" I ask. Uncle Sanjay and Toni keep chatting in the front. "Are they really whales? What do they eat?"

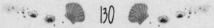

"They're called killer whales, but they're actually in the dolphin family," Hawk says. "They eat fish, and sea lions, and sometimes even whales. They're around twenty-five feet long and can weigh up to six tons."

"Six tons!"

"Yeah, like maybe twelve trucks."

"Whoa."

When we reach West Bluff, a windy park perched over the churning Pacific Ocean, we take the dogs out on leashes; then we all sit at a picnic table, the wind whipping our hair, and eat our peanut butter and lavender chutney sandwiches. We take turns with the binoculars, watching the sea. We search the waves for almost an hour. Just when I think the orcas won't ever come, I see the fins.

"There, look!" They're silver and shiny in the sun, arching through the ocean.

"Whoa, cool," Hawk says. "I'll have to check with the research center and see if this is J-pod. I can't tell by looking."

Toni's lashes flutter. She closes her eyes and sways. I wonder if she is reading the thoughts of orcas.

The sky brightens. The orcas weave in close to the shore, and then they head north. The sounds of nature flood into me—the chatter of birds, the rustle of leaves, the whistle of the wind. The sea stretches away, and I

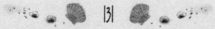

131

think of everything that hides in its depths. Octopuses, sharks, sea urchins, shipwrecks—all the secrets that live and die underneath the water, never stepping on land, never looking a human in the eye.

On the way home, we're all tired, and my skin smells like sea salt. The ocean, so full of life, calmed me. Maybe somewhere, Marmalade really is playing. I still feel his warmth, his fur.

"Hey, Poppy," Hawk says. He taps his finger on the window control. "Wanna, um, go bike riding with me tomorrow? I gotta put up flyers for my mom. She's selling her old beat-up car."

"I don't have a bike."

"Oh, come on. I bet your uncle has one. Doc!"

Uncle Sanjay turns around, his cheeks flushed, his hair blown back by the wind. "I've got a bicycle, my dear niece. Just for you."

chapter twenty-four
LITTLE CHICK

Uncle Sanjay's bike belongs in a museum display of ancient wheeled contraptions from the dawn of time. I'm surprised the wobbly seat doesn't fall off. Rust is munching away at the metal, and I have only one gear. First gear for going uphill, first gear for going downhill, first gear for flat ground.

"I haven't ridden this hump of tin since my earliest days in Virginia," Uncle Sanjay says, patting the seat. At least the tires aren't flat, and there's a basket attached to the handlebars.

"This will be fine," I say. Fine if you lived about a thousand years ago. I drop a bottle of water into the basket. "Do the brakes work? I don't want to crash."

"I've checked. And wear the helmet. Don't get lost, all right?"

He holds Stu's leash while I pedal away. I wish I could take Stu with me, but he has a mild case of garbage gut. He threw up last night after eating something rotten in the street. He's okay, but Uncle Sanjay wants to keep an eye on him.

Stu whines, and I wave a sad goodbye as I ride down the road. "Stu, I'll miss you!" I blow him kisses, and Stu wags his tail and barks—a high-pitched, *how dare you leave me?* yelp. He'll have to go to the clinic without me today. Poor Stu.

In a moment, I'm around the corner, and Uncle Sanjay's house disappears from sight. I memorized the directions to Hawk's place, five blocks down, two blocks left, three blocks right.

I didn't think any house could be smaller than Uncle Sanjay's. But Hawk's house is barely a garage with windows. A bunch of flowerpots are scattered around the overgrown front yard. A calico cat trots through the grass and disappears around the side of the house.

I lay Uncle Sanjay's rust heap in the grass, since there's no kickstand on the bike, and knock on the front door. A

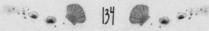

dog barks inside. Hawk shows up at the screen, next to a yapping little black pug with a smashed-in face. Hawk picks up the pug, kisses him, and puts him down. "Stay here for a little while, Gilligan," he says. "I'll be home soon." He steps outside with a pack strapped to his back and shuts the door. "Ready to go? I got the goods. I also have tape and a stapler."

"How many pets do you have?" I ask as I get on my bike.

"Just Gilligan and my cat, Skipper."

"The calico cat?"

Hawk nods. "They get along really well."

I pedal hard to keep up with him on my antique bike. We stop at the Trading Post and staple flyers on the bulletin boards. Hawk's mom is selling her old blue Honda hatchback. We put flyers all over town.

On the way home, we stop for lunch at the Witless Cove Pizzeria. The restaurant buzzes with local people and tourists with cameras slung over their shoulders. We order veggie pizza and cranberry juice and sit at a picnic table outside, next to a bright garden full of flowers and chirping birds. The sun sprinkles through the trees.

"This place has been around forever," Hawk says. "My dad used to bring me here when I was little."

"Where's your dad now?"

"My parents divorced five years ago. He lives in New

Mexico. I fly down to stay with him sometimes."

"Do you ever think about living with him?"

He takes a bite of pizza and talks with his mouth full. "Sometimes I do, but as soon as I'm old enough, I wanna be a technician at Furry Friends. Or a dog whisperer, maybe, like that guy on TV. I dunno. How about you? You still wanna be a vet?"

A brilliant green-blue hummingbird hovers in midair, wings whirring; then it is gone. "Of course I do." But the words come out shaky. Nothing has changed. Nothing at all. But it has. Everything has changed. I'll have to help old kitties die. How many mummified fetuses will I find? But I'll get to save ducks and help puppies be born.

"That's cool," Hawk says. "So you're getting used to the gross stuff."

"Some of it, I guess."

A group of three boys, all about Hawk's age, show up at a nearby picnic table. They're laughing and punching each other in the arm. They're wearing baseball caps backward, and their pants are falling down.

Hawk ducks his head, as if he's trying to avoid them.

"You know those boys?" I ask.

"Kids from town." Hawk turns away from them and shields his eyes against the sun.

"Are they your friends?"

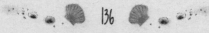 136

"They were all at summer camp. Guess they're back now."

"Didn't you want to go to camp?"

Hawk tears off his pizza crust. "More fun to help at the clinic. Gotta prepare for my future."

"Hey, Hawk!" one of the boys calls out.

Hawk turns around, his face red. "Hey, Johnny!"

The boys look at me and grin, and Johnny waves Hawk over.

Hawk turns into a different person as he strolls over; he swings his arms and hunches his shoulders, trying to be cool, like he doesn't care about a thing in the world.

"Hey, Hawk. How's it goin'?" Johnny says. I catch snippets of their conversation. "Camp" and "movie" and "girls" and "baseball." And "Who's the little chick?"

I'm guessing Johnny is talking about me. I want to tell him I'm not a "little chick," I'm a girl with a name. But I sit quietly, eating my pizza.

"Just a kid . . . ," Hawk says, then lowers his voice. He keeps his back to me, but he doesn't know I have excellent ears. ". . . Doc at the clinic . . . My mom said . . . I gotta babysit her . . . from L.A. . . . ."

The boys laugh.

I nearly spit out my pizza. My face is hot.

Hawk shrugs in my direction, waving an arm, erasing me.

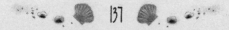 137

Just a kid.

I gotta babysit her.

I get up from the table and throw my paper plate into the garbage. Then I slip around to the front of the pizza parlor, where Hawk and I locked up our bikes. I let the air out of his front tire.

"Hey, Poppy!" Hawk calls out behind me. I don't turn around. I hop onto my bike and ride away, pedaling as fast as I can.

chapter twenty-five
THE BEACH

I hide in my room, and when I know Hawk is working, I stay away from the clinic. Stu and I take many walks on the beach. Two evenings later, the doorbell rings. Uncle Sanjay answers the door.

I hear Hawk's mumbling voice. Maybe his mom sent him.

"Poppy!" Uncle Sanjay calls.

"I'm busy!" I'm under the covers in bed, reading *James Herriot's Cat Stories* by flashlight. I would sit in the closet,

but it's too small. Stu is lying on my feet, farting.

"He says it's urgent," Uncle Sanjay says.

"Tell him to go away." I don't know what could be so important if I'm just a kid he was stuck babysitting.

Uncle Sanjay speaks to Hawk in a low voice; then the front door clicks shut, and Uncle Sanjay comes into my room. "You've had an argument with Hawk, have you? What's going on?"

I pull off the covers, switch off the flashlight, and close my book. "He thinks I'm too young. He wasn't really my friend. He was only pretending. He was *babysitting* me. That's what he told his friends."

Uncle Sanjay sits next to me. "Perhaps he was just showing off. Boys will do that."

"But it was mean." Outside, a sparrow splashes in the birdbath and flies away. There's a new hairline crack in the ceramic bowl.

"I'm sorry, Poppy. Each of us has a dark side, and sometimes we accidentally reveal that dark side to others. Hawk must feel guilty. He apologized."

Stu jumps off the bed and stretches out on the floor.

"I'm not a child anymore. I don't need babysitting."

"No, you don't. You've learned to do so much here already."

"I can weigh a cat by myself, and take a temperature, and walk Stu. I bet I can take the ferry by myself. Pretty soon, I'll be able to fly in a plane by myself, to come back and visit you. Mom and Dad won't have to hold my hand."

Uncle Sanjay reaches down to rub Stu's belly. "That's true, but sometimes it's nice to have other people help you, and it's good to have family and friends who care about you. Hawk appreciates your friendship. He likes you very much, Poppy."

"I don't need him. I have you, and my mom and dad, and Emma and Anna and my other friends back home. And Duff and Stu and the other animals. And I have myself."

"But it's nice to make new friends, nah? Hawk showed you around the clinic. He has helped you, hasn't he?"

"I don't need his help. I'm fine on my own. Pretty soon, his friends won't call me a little chick, because I'll be taller and older. I'll be grown up."

"What's the hurry? Your youth will pass quickly enough. Look at Stu. He's only eight years old, but that's already about forty-five years old in human years. I remember when he was a puppy. Seems as though it was only yesterday."

Stu still acts like a puppy, bouncy and happy.

I pull on a sweater and take him to the beach. The tide is low, the air thick and damp. The shadows of clouds stretch across the sea. A few people are strolling along the waterfront, and here and there, a dog dashes through the surf.

I let Stu off the leash, and he trots along, his nose following invisible scent trails. I find a 1968 penny and a perfect pink cockleshell in the sand. We wander farther and farther, following a curve in the shoreline toward the forest, until we're alone with the seagulls. On a rock that sticks out of the water, an elegant blue heron sits perfectly still. Its long body and beak form curved shadows against the sky.

This is the farthest I've walked on this beach. How long have we been out here? I look back the way we came. I imagine Hawk running toward me, waving his arms, then falling flat on his face at my feet. He'll apologize, and I will turn away.

But nobody's coming. Stu ambles off, climbing across the rocks. I crouch by a tide pool and watch the crabs scuttle through the water. A red starfish clings to a stone. *Look, you can see a whole world in there,* I hear Hawk say. The sky is turning a soft pink at sunset.

"Stu!" I call. "We'd better head back."

He doesn't come. "Stu! Come!" Nothing.

I climb across the rocks. No sign of Stu. I call him again. Where is he? Suddenly, the boulders look jagged. They tumble away for miles along the shoreline.

We wandered too far. It's getting dark. What if Stu is

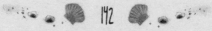

lost? I keep calling for him, searching, and finally, there he is, clambering toward me.

I sigh with relief. "Stu, you nearly gave me a heart attack." But something is wrong. Stu is limping, holding up his left forepaw. "What happened?"

As the heron takes off with a harsh croak, flapping enormous wings, Stu comes nearer. His paw is covered in blood.

CHAPTER TWENTY-SIX
SAVING STU

Stu limps toward me and whines. Blood seeps from a cut on the top of his paw. The sky darkens, and the wind picks up. I glance down the beach—nothing but sand and rocks as far as I can see. I cup my hands around my mouth and yell, "Help! Anybody!" My voice disappears in the wind. "I need help!"

No response.

I grab Stu's collar. "Come up to the grass, or you'll get sand in the wound. Oh, Stu, what did you do?" I should've been watching him. I rush him up the beach to a grassy area at the edge of the forest. He whines all the way.

"It's going to be okay. Don't worry, Stu." My voice shakes. Nobody's on the beach, and it's a long way home. I wish my cell phone worked. I wish I had my veterinarian first-aid kit. Okay, breathe. I have to think about what to do.

I kneel to get a better look at the cut. It's deep. Blood is coming out in a steady stream. A flap of skin hangs off. Stu could bleed to death. I fight nausea. A seagull squawks in the distance. I wish the gull could help. I wish it could carry a message to Uncle Sanjay.

"What do I do?" Put pressure on the wound. With what? Nothing but grass, rocks, and sand on the beach. Leaves? They're too small. I have a tissue in my pocket, but the blood will soak through in a second. Panic rises inside me. I have to use *something*.

I take off my sweater and pull my T-shirt over my head. Then I put my sweater back on and zip it up. I try to rip the shirt, but the fabric is too strong.

"Oh, come on!" I shout to nobody. "Help!" Still no answer. My heart is pounding.

Stu whines more loudly.

"Okay, Stu, it's okay." I fold the T-shirt once, twice, three times. Then I press it to the wound. Stu stays still, as if he knows I'm trying to help him. I press hard. The blood is soaking through. What if the bleeding doesn't stop?

Keep up the pressure, I hear Uncle Sanjay say. *If the blood is spurting, it's probably from an artery . . .* And you apply pressure above the wound.

"The blood isn't spurting. The blood is seeping."

Then it's probably from a vein. Apply pressure below the wound.

I hold the T-shirt with one hand, and I press below the wound with my other hand. "Good boy, Stu," I whisper. "Good boy." Blood covers my fingers. *When you are calm, inside and out, the animal calms down, too.* I imagine the future, the cut all healed. Stu's paw as good as new.

"You're going to be okay." The T-shirt is soaked in blood. What else can I use? I need to clean the wound, but I don't have disinfectant. I wish we could fly to the clinic.

"We need to get you back." I can't carry him. *Wrap the wound from the bottom up.* From the bottom up. Bottom up. I can't use anything on this beach; there are only logs, rocks, seashells, and discarded bottle caps. What can I use? What do I have left? My jeans, my sweater, my underwear. *My socks and shoes.*

The bleeding slows. The T-shirt has begun to stick to the wound. I hold it there with one hand, and with the

146

other, I undo my left shoelace and push off my shoe. I peel off my thick, striped sock.

"Hold still, Stu. This might hurt a bit. Give me your paw." I pull the sock up over Stu's paw, over the T-shirt. The sock fits snugly and holds the T-shirt in place. My hands are clammy. The air grows colder. Inky twilight spills across the sky.

I put my shoe back on over my bare foot. "Come on, we have to go." I clip the leash to his collar, and he limps along beside me. The sand ripples toward me, rising like a wave. I'm going to faint. No, not now. I grab the lavender sachet from my pocket and take a deep whiff. The sweet scent revives me.

Blood seeps through the sock on Stu's paw, so I stop and pull my other sock over the first one. "We're almost there. Come on." He looks up at me with those deep brown eyes, and I know he believes me. He's relying on me. I can't let him down. But the long way back takes forever, as if we are walking across the entire planet.

Then I see a tall, dark shape running toward us, feet pointing sideways, hair sticking out in every direction. "Uncle Sanjay!" I shout.

"My dear niece! Stu! What on Earth has happened?"

Chapter Twenty-seven
HAWK

At the clinic, Uncle Sanjay cleans the wound and closes it with tissue glue. Then he wraps Stu's paw in a bandage from the bottom up. Stu suffers through his treatment with quiet patience; then he limps to the office to drink from his water bowl. Then he eats. Then he farts and goes out back in the darkness to poop. He limps back in and stays close to me.

"You did well, my dear niece," Uncle Sanjay says. "You did a wonderful job of improvising. If you hadn't kept

pressure on the wound, Stu would've been in bad shape."

"I should've been watching him every second."

"We can't prevent every bad thing from happening in the world. Dogs cut their paws all the time. Stu must've stepped in glass, but I didn't find any in the wound."

"I shouldn't have walked that far."

"I should've gone with you. But you did well on your own."

The next morning everyone at the clinic overwhelms Stu with kisses and hugs. Saundra brings him lavender biscuits.

Hawk gives him a new chew toy. "Wanna go for a walk to the beach, Poppy?"

"I don't need a babysitter."

"I know. I just want to talk."

I hesitate. "But Stu can't come."

"It's okay. He's happy here." Stu limps around, wagging his tail, basking in love and sympathy.

"Okay. Fine."

When we get to the beach, Hawk says, "I hear your parents are coming all the way out here to get you."

"In three days."

"Are you gonna come back? Maybe next summer?"

"Yeah. I want to." The island spills over with life—

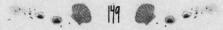

149

leaves rustling, birds chattering, and the sea rushing.

"I'm glad Stu's okay," Hawk says.

"Me too," I say.

"Hey, I didn't mean what I said, about you being just a kid."

"Yeah, I know."

"We could go out in a boat next time you're here. My friend's dad owns a yacht, takes it around the islands."

"We could see J-pod up close, maybe?"

"If you spot killer whales from a boat, you have to cut the engine and drift, and you can't get too close."

"That would be awesome." We walk near the waterline. The tide is going out, leaving new seashells embedded in the damp sand.

"When do you go back to school?" Hawk asks.

"The end of August."

"We start in September. I go to Island Middle School."

"I go to Coast Elementary in Santa Monica. But I wish I could stay here a few more weeks."

"Me too. Next summer, I could show you more beaches up north. There's a lot to see on this island. There's some cool stuff at the maritime museum. Sea cucumbers, a whale skeleton, and some gross stuff. You might faint."

I grin. "When I'm not here, who will you tease?"

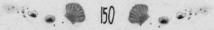

He shrugs. "I'll wait for you, I guess."

I turn the seaglass around in the sun, study the small speckles trapped inside. Maybe they're dust, or dirt, or tiny fish tears. I can't know for sure. All I know is I don't need the glass anymore. I throw it into the waves for someone else to find.

Chapter Twenty-eight
TIME MARCHES FORWARD

In the morning, I'm up early. I arrive at the Trading Post the moment the store opens. I buy a sympathy card with a picture of a brown tabby cat and *We'd like to believe they'll be with us forever* on the front. Inside are the words . . . *and in our hearts, they are.* I can't find a card with a picture of an orange cat, and anyway, it wouldn't be Marmalade.

I write, *Dear Mr. Pincus, I know what Marmalade is doing in the next world. He's meowing at birds and eating jam.*

Then I end with what other people usually write: *I'm so sorry for your loss.* But "sorry" doesn't seem like enough.

I slip my lavender pillow into the envelope; then I ride Uncle Sanjay's antique bike through town, the salty sea breeze in my face. Mr. Pincus lives in a two-story house made of wood and tall windows. I park my bike in the driveway and run up the steps to the front door. Cat wind chimes dangle from the eaves, and a carved wooden kitten sits by the door, batting at imaginary butterflies. Mr. Pincus answers the door in a robe and slippers.

"Oh, did I wake you up?" I ask. "I know it's still early—"

"Poppy, what a pleasant surprise. Please, come on in." He steps back to let me inside. His house is made for cats; toys, kitty condos, and scratching posts are everywhere. Pictures of Marmalade cover the walls. Marmalade in the garden, Marmalade sleeping on a blanket, Marmalade with his head in a jar of marmalade.

"Won't you have something to drink?" he asks.

"I, um, just wanted to give you this." I hand him the envelope.

"For me? You're very kind." He opens the envelope, takes out my lavender pillow, and sniffs. "Ah, I never get tired of that fragrance." Then he reads the card, and his

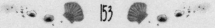 153

eyes fill with tears. "Oh, my Marmalade." He presses his hand to his chest.

I swallow tears. "I'll always remember him. Forever and ever." Outside, on the deck, a flock of yellow birds lands on a tray of birdseed.

"Come, I want to show you something." Mr. Pincus leads me out into the backyard, into a sunny garden of colorful flowers and leafy plants. In the center of the garden is a white rock with words painted in orange:

In Memory of Marmalade

"I planted catnip all around the edges," Mr. Pincus says. Tears stream down his cheeks. "He loved catnip."

We stand there for a few minutes, silently remembering Marmalade, and then we go back inside.

"Would you like to see the newest members of my family?" Mr. Pincus says, wiping his eyes. "They're still getting used to their new home."

"New family members?" I blink.

He motions me to follow him down the hall, a finger pressed to his lips. "Stay quiet. They get spooked easily."

At the end of the hall, a door is ajar. He pushes it open. On a fluffy bed, a white cat is curled up, staring

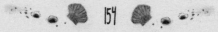

at me through nervous green eyes. A black cat sits on the headboard, flicking its tail.

"Hansel and Gretel!" I say. "But—"

"I adopted them a few days ago. Toni rescued new foster cats, so she asked me to take these two."

Hansel hops onto the floor, trots toward me, and rubs against my legs. I pick him up and pet him.

Mr. Pincus smiles. "See, he likes you. Gretel's still nervous. This is her safe room. Hansel is a bit bolder. Come on."

I put Hansel down, and we tiptoe back down the hall. Hansel follows us. "I'm glad you adopted new kitties," I say. Mr. Pincus won't be so lonely now.

"I'll never forget Marmalade. He'll always hold a special place in my heart. I will always love him. Nothing will ever replace him. But these kitties needed a home right away. I couldn't say no."

On my way down the street, I pass a man jogging in shorts and a Nisqually Island T-shirt, a girl walking a poodle, and a lady pushing a stroller with a round-faced baby inside. They all wave at me, and I wave back.

I'm beginning to know my way around these streets with Northwest names—Chinook Place, Samish Street, Orca Lane, Witless Cove Road. I love the cool, salty breeze, the sound of the surf, the call of seabirds, the way each day is different. Some mornings, mist rolls in from

the sea; sometimes the rains come; and sometimes the sun shines warm and bright.

Before turning the corner, I glance back at Mr. Pincus's tall wooden house. As the sun rises higher, the windows begin to reflect the swaying trees, the sky, and the clouds speeding by, on their way to somewhere new.

Chapter Twenty-nine
LEAVING

Doris brings Shopsy back to the clinic to be groomed. His hair is growing again, and his skin infection is gone. I comb him carefully. He's still small and fragile, but I'm no longer afraid of hurting him. When I finish, he looks beautiful, if a bit patchy.

"Nice job, Poppy," Saundra says.

Harvey brings Bremolo back for another checkup. He's trotting along at top speed. "He doesn't need the pain meds anymore," Harvey says. "He's started

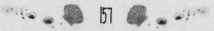

hopping up and down the stairs. You saved his life."

"That's my job." Uncle Sanjay gives Bremolo a treat, and the little dog struts around, wagging his curly tail. Even Saundra smiles at him.

Lulu comes back, too, her golden hair flying. Mrs. Lopez runs after her, calling, "Lulu, get back here! Oh, Lulu!"

Lulu stops and squats; Hawk cleans up her pee; and then she and Bremolo and Stu dash around the hospital together. "I'm so sorry!" Mrs. Lopez says. "She loves everyone, you see."

I get to see Droopy and Francine one more time, when Toni brings Francine back with another eye infection. Uncle Sanjay gives her the medicine for free.

On my last afternoon at the clinic, Saundra throws a bon voyage party for me. She gives me the oversized lab coat. "For when you become a vet. You'll grow into it."

Duff gives me a dog brush, and Hawk gives me a chunk of white quartz.

"We're gonna miss you, Poppy," Duff says. "Now I have to weigh the cats by myself."

"I'm going to miss you, too." I hug everyone.

The next morning, Hawk comes over for breakfast. He hangs out in the backyard, petting Stu while Uncle Sanjay cooks up samosas and eggs. Oil splatters all over his glasses.

I give him a big hug. "I'm going to miss your cooking."

"My cooking will miss you, too." He gives me a soft smile.

Outside, birds twitter in the garden. I've grown to enjoy their song, and I even rescued a spider last night. I scooped her into my hand and dropped her in the garden. Her hairy legs didn't scare me.

I sit at the kitchen table and rest my chin in my hands. "I don't want to leave, Uncle. I wish I could take the island home."

"I wish you could stay. I'll come and visit you soon, and perhaps you'll come back next summer?"

"Every summer. And you know what? No matter what Dadu ever said, I think you're the greatest vet on the planet, better than Dr. Dolittle."

He gives me a startled smile. "Thank you, my dear niece. I have a present for you—a memento of your stay." A small box wrapped in brown paper in a Trading Post shopping bag. "Don't open it until you get home. Keep it well cushioned."

I pack the gift in my suitcase, wrapped in two sweaters.

When my parents show up, my regular life comes flooding back to me, but it feels like a different life now. The smog and freeways and noisy traffic of Los Angeles have become a strange, faraway world. My days and nights on Nisqually Island, the furballs, worms in jars, newborn puppies, and ancient cats—the messiness

159

and joy and sadness all feel like my real life.

I could stay here forever, with my new island family and friends, but my heart leaps as Mom emerges from the passenger side of the car, Dad from the driver's side. My parents look smaller and thinner than before. Mom is wearing a new loose Indian shirt painted in bright flowers, and a colorful bead necklace. Her bangles jingle and clink. Dad's white shirt is rumpled, his hair a little messier than usual.

Uncle Sanjay steps out onto the porch and waves. Hawk stands in the yard, throwing the ball and catching it. Stu gingerly prances back and forth, staring hopefully at the ball.

Mom rushes over and hugs me. "We missed you so much. We've brought you some presents. Everyone asked about you."

Stu limps over and jumps on Mom, knocking her back into the grass. She sneezes once, twice.

"Studebaker Chatterji!" I yell, pulling him off. "Bad dog. No jumping."

"It's all right." Mom gets up and brushes off her clothes.

Uncle Sanjay runs down the steps and clips the leash to Stu's collar. "I'm so sorry—"

"So good to see you." Mom hugs Uncle Sanjay. "What a lovely cottage! I wish we could go inside, but I'll never stop sneezing."

"Poppykins!" Dad rushes toward me, lifts me up, and presses wet kisses to my cheeks. "What have you been up to, my grown-up girl?"

"Oh, Dad, I have so much to tell you."

"She'll have many stories to share," Uncle Sanjay says, hugging Dad. Mom's eyes are watering, and her nose turns pink from all the sneezing.

"Next time you come, you can stay at the Witless Cove Motel," Uncle Sanjay says. "No pets allowed there."

Stu's tail wags a mile a minute.

"Here, I'll take him," Hawk says. He dashes over, grabs the leash, and steers Stu away from my mom.

"This is my friend Hawk," I say. "He showed me around the clinic, and the beaches, and the town."

Hawk grins at me.

"Lovely to meet you!" Mom says. Dad nods at him and smiles.

"We've brought you some tea," Mom says to Uncle Sanjay. "Darjeeling, first flush. Your favorite."

Uncle Sanjay's eyes twinkle with happiness. "Come come, we can all sit at the picnic table in the backyard. I'm afraid the house is full of Stu's hair. You're better off out here."

Mom opens her arms and takes a deep breath. "Smell the freshness. Isn't it wonderful, Poppy?"

"Beautiful," I say. "It's Nisqually Island air."

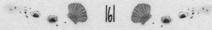

Chapter Thirty
HOME AGAIN

Back home in my room, I hang the lab coat in my closet. Mom and Dad brought me sandalwood soap, jewelry, and cotton kurta shirts from India. They also gave me a brand-new veterinarian first-aid kit. I donated it to the local humane society. I have plenty of time to learn how to use the tools of a veterinarian. Sometimes, you don't need all that equipment anyway. You need your mind, your heart, and steady hands. And maybe a T-shirt and a pair of socks.

But I keep my original, battered first aid kit, the one that fell into the stream. The plastic is cracked, the hinges busted. But even a broken box can be useful. I put it on my bookshelf. Inside, I arrange my treasures from Nisqually Island, including the dog brush, chunks of white quartz, ridged pink cockleshells, a 1968 penny, and a bouquet of dried lavender.

Downstairs, Mom is singing, clinking dishes in the kitchen. She is making *mishti doi*, my favorite Bengali yogurt, for dessert. Dad is outside, pressure washing the concrete driveway. Across the street, kids are shouting and playing. Traffic rushes in the distance, and the afternoon sunlight slants across my bed, but I am not quite all the way home. Part of me is still in Witless Cove, petting Bremolo, hugging Stu, walking in Marmalade's garden.

I open Uncle Sanjay's present, an empty spice bottle made of clear glass. Well, not empty. The bottle is labeled GENUINE WITLESS COVE AIR. I'll return to the island to feel the salty sea breeze on my face, to ride bikes along shady lanes, to explore the beaches with Hawk. Until then, I will keep the jar on my windowsill, where I can see it every day.

ACKNOWLEDGMENTS

I'm grateful to Monet, my beloved cat, who followed me around, slept next to me every night, and sat on my lap while I wrote this book. His death was sudden and unexpected. I wish I could've said goodbye. He joins the spirits of the other animals I have loved and lost—Shanti the cat, Whitely the dog, Friday the rabbit, and more. Thanks to the robin that first brought out my compassion. When I was eight years old, my friends and I dressed in our Sunday bests, buried him under a makeshift wooden cross, and held an elaborate garden memorial service.

I'm also grateful to Dr. Tara Nanavati, the James Herriot of the town of Seymour, Connecticut. I learned of him from an article in *India Abroad* magazine. Dr. Nanavati has dedicated his life to helping animals, although he knows vets are a "neglected lot."

My editor, Wendy Lamb, helped me brainstorm the book. I'm thankful for her support. She wouldn't give up on me and ultimately helped me find the true story here. I would not have found my way without her and the primary editor for this book, Caroline Meckler. Infinitely patient, Caroline has helped me craft my work with the finesse of a master. Thanks also to the rest of the Random House team, including the wonderful copy editors, and Marci Senders for her brilliant design. I'm also grateful to Jodi Reamer.

My deepest gratitude to my wonderful Bainbridge Island fellow writers—Susan Wiggs, Carol Cassella, Sheila Rabe, Elsa Watson, and Suzanne Selfors. Special thanks to Susan for her last-minute read of Chapter One and for helping choose the book title. Without her, I would have been lost.

Thanks to Dr. David Parent, DVM, and his staff at the Useless Bay Animal Clinic in Freeland, Washington.

Special, heartfelt thanks to Carol Ann Morris, DVM, beloved friend and veterinarian, and her wonderful associates at Belfair Animal Hospital—Shannon Stewart, Jaci Peifer, Niki Day, Lisa O'Donnell, and the hospital owner, Dr. Gary Sleight. Thank you for allowing me to sit in on appointments and for sharing your stories.

Way back when, I worked with Alan and Nancy Kay, DVMs, at the Oakland Veterinary Hospital in California. My experience there gave me texture for this story as well.

My friend Susan Neal contributed some great brainstorming.

Thanks also to my Silverdale writing group: Jim Gullo, Skip Morris, Penny Percenti, Sherill Leonardi, Cassandra

Firman, and Mike Donnelly. Special thanks to Kate Breslin and Janine Donoho for reading a late-stage version of the manuscript, and to Uma Krishnaswami, for her wise feedback. Karen Brown and Kristin Von Kreisler gave me thoughtful input at the last minute.

I can't forget Lois Faye Dyer and Rose Marie Harris for in-depth discussions while swimming at the Parkwood Community Club pool. Many thanks to Gitana Garofalo, Vito Zingarelli, Amy Wheeler, M. Louise McKay, and everyone at Hedgebrook, an idyllic retreat for women writers on Whidbey Island.

Members of my Friday Tea group gave me some great ideas—thanks to Terrel Hoffman, Carol Wissmann, Jan Symonds, Dee Marie, Toni Bonnell, Sandra Hill, Soudabeh Pourarien, Jana Bourne, and Elizabeth Corcoran Murray. My "title brainstormers"—Brenda Gurung, Kari Yadro, Ada Con, Justina Chen Headley, Mitali Perkins, and Mary Palmer—provided much-needed perspective.

As always, I thank my husband, Joseph; my mom, Denise, for her insight; and my stepdad, Randy, for his encouraging laughter at scenes read aloud. Thanks to my family for their support, and of course to our wonderful cats—Luna, Cheyenne, Simon, and Ruby.

AnJali BanerJee is the author of *Maya Running* and *Looking for Bapu*, as well as books for adults. She was born in India, grew up in Canada and California, and received degrees from the University of California, Berkeley. At the age of seven, she wrote her first story, about an abandoned puppy she found on a beach in Bengal. She lives in the Pacific Northwest with her husband and four crazy cats. Learn more about Anjali on her Web site, www.anjalibanerjee.com.